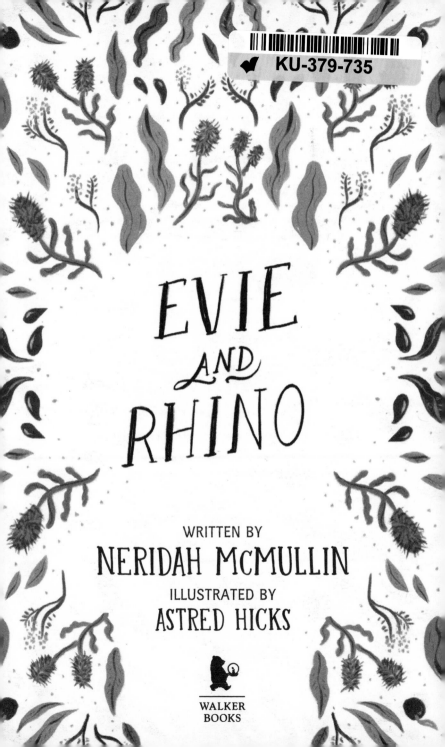

EVIE AND RHINO

WRITTEN BY

NERIDAH McMULLIN

ILLUSTRATED BY

ASTRED HICKS

WALKER BOOKS

First published in Great Britain 2023 by Walker Books Ltd
87 Vauxhall Walk, London SE11 5HJ

2 4 6 8 10 9 7 5 3 1

Text © 2022 Neridah McMullin
Illustrations © 2022 Astred Hicks

The right of Neridah McMullin to be identified as author
of this work has been asserted in accordance with
the Copyright, Designs and Patents Act 1988

This book has been typeset in IvyJournal

Printed and bound by CPI Group (UK) Ltd, Croydon CR0 4YY

British Library Cataloguing in Publication Data:
a catalogue record for this book is available from the British Library

ISBN 978-1-5295-1115-4

www.walker.co.uk

MIX
Paper | Supporting
responsible forestry
FSC® C171272

TO MY PARENTS, JOHN AND LYNETTE,
FOR THE BEST CHILDHOOD

CHAPTER 1

14 JULY 1891, CAPE OTWAY

The animals have been at sea for two months, kept in makeshift cages on the deck of the steamship *SS Bancoora*. The ship never ceases its swaying and rolling and the animals can't keep their feet. They're wet and cold and bruised and a sense of hopelessness hangs in the air.

There are six rhesus monkeys, a rhinoceros, two white cranes and six exotic green parrots. There was a young elephant, but without her mother for milk she perished soon after sailing from Calcutta.

In the first few weeks, the monkeys and the birds chattered and screeched. But the birds now shiver, featherless from plucking themselves out of anxiety, and the monkeys groan with seasickness.

If Rhino tilts his head at a certain angle, he can see the monkeys through the bars of his stall. He hums from deep inside his belly to calm them, to try to reassure them all will be well.

In the darkness of night, the monkeys reach into his cage and touch his horn and stroke his hairy ears. He licks their cold, icy little hands, and huffs on them.

They may be of different species, animals he wouldn't associate with in the wild, but out here, desperate with fear, they've bonded.

It's a moonless night and Rhino can feel the weather changing. He can smell it in the air. The wind is picking up and the sea begins to chop and churn.

No one sees the wave rise above them like a mountain. The tip curls and a massive wall of water smashes down upon them. The ship bounces wildly in the water. Rhino's ears pop and squeak. The monkeys scream and the birds screech as they're smashed against the sides of their cages.

Rhino braces himself against the bars of his stall, and above the roaring noise of the storm he calls and moos to comfort his friends. The animals are tossed and battered around in their cages until their screams are barely a whimper.

People are running around on deck. Lanterns flash yellow and red.

Suddenly, Rhino jolts forward, smacking his head into the bars of his stall. Stars of white light dance before his eyes, his head throbs with pain and his ears ring.

The ship makes a deep mawing, scraping sound. It shudders, then Rhino hears a tearing noise that's raw and wounded. He doesn't know what it is, but it's the most sorrowful, awful thing he's ever heard. It tugs at his heart. When the planks under his feet begin to move and pop and buckle, he knows they're in grave danger.

The humans scream at each other and the wind whips away their words. Nobody knows what they're meant to be doing and they tumble across the deck as the rain lashes down.

One of the keepers, the kindest of them all, appears dripping and shivering before Rhino. He tries to prise open the cages but his fingers slip and fumble. Rhino can see the whites of his eyes. He can smell his fear.

"Leave the animals. Save yourself!" cries a human, and he launches himself overboard.

One by one, the cages are flung open by the kindest human. Rhino tries to charge from the listing deck, but he hasn't used his legs for months and they're tingling and wobbly.

Rhino sees the monkeys, light as banana leaves, picked up by the wind and tossed overboard. As he staggers and lolls, fighting to keep his balance, he topples backwards into the black icy sea.

Sinking into darkness, Rhino dreams of his mother. His memories of her have faded over the years, but she comes to him now. He can hear her, feel her and smell her grassy breath.

His lungs start to burn and his heart thuds like a drum. Something is calling to him, calling his name. Eventually, he starts kicking his legs, slowly and uncoordinated, then more strongly until he breaks the surface of the sea.

He gasps at the cold, fresh air, free of the stench and filth of the cage. The sea spray is blinding but he senses the monkeys are near, he can hear them

splashing. They're paddling in circles not far away. He moos to them and they swim to him. Clambering onto his nose, they scream and chatter, clutching at his face.

Rhino can't see a thing and he tosses his head, shuffling the monkeys down his neck, where they cling onto his back.

The birds are overhead, screeching and flapping their wings, trying to stay aflight against the wind.

Despite his weakened state, Rhino is a strong swimmer. His nostrils flare; he can smell the warmth of the earth to the north. He starts to paddle and soon settles into a steady rhythm, swimming towards landfall.

After what feels like an eternity, Rhino can see the light changing from a dull grey to a peachy gold. Dawn is nearing. The wind is easing and the swell begins to calm.

The sea has become flat and glassy, as if it too is exhausted from the storm.

Rhino's legs are cramping with weariness but he pushes onwards. The monkeys have long stopped their crying and he can feel their little bodies shivering against him.

Rhino is nearly spent when one of his feet hits the sandy bottom. He paddles on until all four are touching the sand. He catches his breath and moos to wake the monkeys. He can feel them stirring and they start to chatter.

Rhino wades in through the surf and into the shallows, ploughing one weary foot in front of the other until he crashes heavily onto the beach.

The monkeys leap off Rhino. They stagger upon the sand, hopping on tippy-toes from one foot to the other. Uncertain of their surroundings, they cast darting looks, chittering and chattering. They make a decision and, grabbing one another by the hands, they scurry off into the marram grass-covered sand dunes.

Rhino sighs as he feels the warmth of the morning sun on his back. He's remembering another time in another place, far, far away. He imagines what he's been through is just a nightmare. He dreams of the smell of spices and of tea and cows and chickens.

His eyelids droop like heavy shutters and he falls sound asleep in the shallows.

CHAPTER 2

15 JULY 1891, BREAMLEA

Evie runs through the garden. She's fairy-light on her feet as she follows a path from Lunar House to the beach. Grandpa's two Smithfield dogs, Francie and Freddie, have heard her. They know she's going on one of her walks and they're on her scent, racing each other to catch up. The birds are full of voice. Evie can hear robins and wrens and warbling magpies.

Bursting from the undergrowth, she races through the paddocks, under the rustling moonah trees. She touches their weathered grey trunks, bent and twisted by the wind. It's been raining for five weeks and it's the first morning Evie's been able to get outside again. It feels heavenly. Arriving at the sand dunes, she inhales the scent of the earth after rain, a heady mixture of eucalyptus and ocean.

Evie counts the clumps of marram grass as she climbs the dunes. Her sturdy boots stomp and her woollen dress swooshes around her heavily stockinged legs. She dresses for practicality, with not a trim or a frill in sight. Being warm against icy winds and sea spray takes priority, as does her jacket, chosen for its impressively deep pockets, deep enough for her to fill with shells and sea sponges and treasures she finds on her walks.

Evie stops counting at ten. *The same age as me.* Small and willowy, her hair is long, blonde and wildly unkept. Her face is heart-shaped with two perfect dimples in her cheeks. Her eyes are the vibrant blue of the sea, but there are dark depths that hint at sadness.

It's been two years since Evie's parents drowned in a shipwreck at Cape Otway in south west Victoria. Since then, she's lived with her grandpa, Charlie Strahan, at Lunar House. He understands Evie and she understands him. They both understand the light and dark of this world, and they get by the best they can.

Evie hasn't spoken a word in two years. It suited her at first. How could she express the aching, black emptiness inside of her? But it's gone on for too long, and she worries if she opens her mouth now, she might shatter into a million pieces.

Lunar House was grandly built by Grandma Amelie in 1849, named after her ancestral home in Scotland. It's big, old and crumbling now, with only Grandpa and Evie living there. Yes, it's seen better days. Now it is dark and damp, but not gloomy. The people who dwell within are not cold.

The house has a pleasing, balanced symmetry, with the same number of windows on each of its three stories. With twelve bedrooms, six bathrooms, two dining rooms, a huge ballroom, a billiard room, two sitting rooms, a study and a library, you'd think Evie would have trouble trying to find her way around, but it's quite the opposite.

Lunar House is not just any house. It's a living, breathing being. Evie feels every creak and groan and sigh as an embrace. It shudders and rattles in winter, but she feels it talking to her, reassuring her and reminding her. Reminding her of the ones they've loved and lost. It is home, a refuge for Evie and Grandpa, a place they feel safe together.

A kilometre inland, Lunar House sits between sand dunes to the south and Bream Creek to the north. It is isolated and windswept, but stands with a firm solidarity.

Most of the bedrooms are closed up for winter. The dining rooms are covered in dustsheets, and in the disused ballroom the ceiling leaks and chunks of plaster crumble from its ornate cornices. When Grandma Amelie passed away twenty years ago, Grandpa lost interest in its upkeep. He lost interest in everything. Except his birds. Grandpa is an ornithologist, an expert in the scientific study of birds, and he's always asking Evie what she sees on her walks. It's become a part of her now. She's excellent at watching and listening.

Francie and Freddie appear, their pink tongues lolling with slobber. They tumble over each other to get to Evie. She stops them in their tracks by holding an open palm in front of them. Pointing her index finger she makes them "sit". They do, even though their bottoms are wriggling in the sand. She ruffles their velvety ears before they take off again, racing on ahead of her.

Evie puffs and pants until she reaches the top of the sand dune.

WHOOSH!

A south-easterly gale greets her and nearly flips her backwards. She leans into the wind, reaching her arms high above. The wind snaps at her hair and tears stream from her eyes. After a few moments, Evie throws herself over the edge of the dune, rolling all the way down to the beach. She loves tumbling down the dunes.

Evie brushes off the sand and walks to the water's edge. She drops to her knees and places her hands on her heart. She gazes out past the break,

beyond the green rolling surf to an open ocean, icy and black.

How she longs for her mama and papa. But out here, at least she can feel something, even if it's the chill of the wind. She closes her eyes and listens.

I know you're out there, Mama. I know you're out there, Papa. I can feel you.

The storm has washed in masses of seaweed and kelp. A salty tang fills the air and the dogs madly sniff and snuffle.

Evie picks up a piece of driftwood. She wades in to look at a length of timber floating in and out with the waves. She touches it. It's not waterlogged,

and there are no barnacles, which means it hasn't been in the water very long.

Then she sees a tell-tale sign on the timber: a streak of smeared tar. Tar caulking makes ships watertight. An uneasy feeling washes over Evie. She breathes in short gasps. Further along the shallows, she finds an oak barrel, a length of tangled rope and clothes floating in the water. That's when she knows for sure – there's been a shipwreck!

Evie sprints along the beach to see if there are any survivors.

A dark mass looms on the beach in the distance. Evie stops. Puffing hard, she tries to make it out. *What is it?* It looks like a bull seal, but the shape of it is all wrong. As Evie runs, the dark thing becomes bigger and bigger. Francie and Freddie have seen it too and they're racing ahead of her.

Is it a whale? Evie's seen plenty of them, but they don't look anything like this.

Evie's heart quivers in her chest as she nears the creature. *What is it?*

Francie and Freddie are whining, and stalking around it in a wide arc.

Evie can see the creature's legs are beneath it and it appears to be sleeping in the shallows. *Or is it dead?* She's not sure it's breathing.

The dogs throw up their heads and howl, then tear off home with their tails between their legs.

Evie stops in front of the creature. Her heart leaps high in her chest; she's never seen anything like it. It's huge! Its skin is like armour, thick and grey-brown with pinkish skinfolds. Its legs and shoulders have wart-like bumps all over and it has small ears fringed with spiky hair. Evie can see it's hurt – there are cuts all over its body.

The creature's head is misshapen, with a single huge horn rising from the bridge of its nose. Its eyes are closed, with long curling eyelashes encrusted with salt.

Kneeling in the sand, Evie shuffles closer to the creature. Softly, and ever so gently, she lays her hand on its cheek. An electric shock shivers up her arm. It's warm – it's alive! She watches until she sees the gentle rise and fall of its flanks.

Evie leans down at eye level with the creature. Staring at it, she sends a message. *You're going to be all right. I'm going to help you. My grandpa will help you.*

Just then, an eyelid flutters open. Evie jerks backward. The eye staring back at her is bloodshot and red-rimmed and it blinks several times.

CHAPTER 3

Lying on her stomach with her elbows wedged in the sand, Evie finds herself staring into warm, brown, intelligent eyes. And then the strangest thing happens. The creature curls its lip into a grin. Evie smiles, knowing in her heart it's full of kindness.

She reaches out and rubs its neck. The creature smacks its lips together and moos at Evie.

Did it just moo at me? Like a cow?

Evie grins; it's such an unexpected sound. The creature grins at Evie. It licks its lips again and closes its eyes, lowering its head down onto the sand, exhausted.

It's thirsty, realises Evie. She leaps to her feet.

Her dress is damp and heavy. Regardless, she runs all the way home, heading for the stables. She grabs a bucket and dunks it in a water trough, filling it to the brim.

As Evie trudges back up the sand dunes, her arms and legs are burning from the weight of the bucket. She puffs and pants and staggers down the other side, determined not to spill a drop.

Running along the beach is easy compared to on the dunes and at last she arrives back at the shallows to find the creature is still asleep.

Evie tilts the bucket and drips some over the edge and onto the creature's nose so it knows it's fresh water. It does the trick and the creature lifts its weary head. With a grunt and a groan, it half sits up, towering above her. She grins and holds up the water bucket. It lowers its head and drinks, taking long slurps and rhythmic swallows. It pauses to look at Evie. Remaining very still, it delivers her a great, despairing stare, which Evie recognises immediately. She sees what's in the creature's eyes as if they were mirrors. Her own truth is staring right back at her. Evie strokes the creature on the nose. They understand each other.

With a shock, Rhino glimpses his own sadness reflected in the eyes of the golden-haired human child. Her heart is full of an aching blackness, which he recognises. She, too, understands pain and loss. A tiny flicker of hope ignites inside him and he knows he can trust this human child with his life. He burps before lowering his head again to drink.

The child reaches up and touches his horn. She taps it with her finger and clicks her tongue, encouraging him to rise. He doesn't want to get up, but he does, for her, and he groans as he struggles to stand on his wobbly feet.

As Rhino is led by his horn by the human child, he swirls his little tail in the air, and farts.

CHAPTER 4

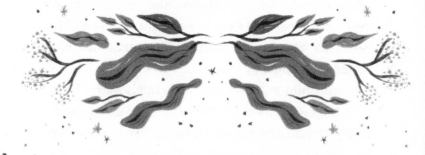

It isn't easy getting the creature up and over the sand dunes. Evie lets it rest at the top, but it grunts and groans and pants like a dog. Then it moans and tumbles down the other side, kicking sand everywhere. They sit at the bottom, smiling at each other, spitting out gritty mouthfuls of sand. The creature rests briefly before heaving itself up again.

Francie and Freddie are skulking in the garden but the creature ignores them and plods on. Through hooded eyes, he staggers into the stables.

The chickens scatter, but curiosity gets the better of them and, led by Albine, they soon come back for a stickybeak.

Albine is a plump, black-and-white speckled, sweet-natured Cochin chicken. She tries to mother everyone, especially Evie. Their housekeeper, Cook, gave in to Evie having a chicken in the house, but under no uncertain terms are chickens allowed in her bedroom. They're strictly out of bounds.

The creature sways on his feet with exhaustion. Evie picks up a pitchfork and prepares a straw bed for him in the far stall. It's the foaling stall and it's never used these days. Grandpa gave away breeding horses, so there hasn't been a birth in years. Albine and the ladies pick and peck around him. He gently snuffles them, blowing air out of his nostrils as if

he's introducing himself. The ladies *burk burk*, making a fuss.

Grandpa says chickens are always good judges of character. Evie can see the ladies are far from scared of the creature.

When Evie finishes making the bed, she leads the creature forward. He collapses with a huff onto the clean, soft straw and she fills the water bucket for him and he gulps it down. She returns to the trough eleven more times until he unleashes an enormous burp before lying down.

Evie gathers hay from the loft, but by the time she returns he's snuffling in his sleep. She leaves the hay close by, in case the creature awakes hungry. The ladies perch on the railing above, clucking softly.

Evie hurries into the house to find Grandpa, but Cook, their extraordinary cook, is blocking the doorway.

"Cook from the 'eart, I do. From me mother and me grandmother and me grandmother's mother. It's all in 'ere," she often says, tapping her temple and then her heart.

Cook is grandmotherly, short and rotund and she wears her apron like a shield. She can be brisk and matter-of-fact, but her heart is as soft as a feather-down pillow. Cook believes a cup of tea and a slice of apple pie can fix just about anything. Her pies are full of sticky, syrupy apples, which are sweet and tangy at the same time, wrapped in a golden crust pastry and sprinkled with sugar. Cook's cups of tea can cure a variety of ailments from shock to indigestion to the common cold. But she still doesn't like Evie getting soaked with rain.

"Yer wet again, child. Look at yer! Yer'll catch yer death of a cold."

Evie shakes her head and Cook reaches down and feels her stockings.

"Yer drenched. Come on, let's git yer changed," she sighs. "Again."

Despite Cook's regular scoldings, Evie knows they come from a good place. Cook is always making sure Evie doesn't catch her "death of a cold" and tells her how grateful she is for her help around the farm. Cook and the house cow, Dominique, don't get on. So Evie milks "that daft cow" for her and collects the chicken eggs, and leaves them in the pantry.

"The apple doesn't fall far from the tree," Cook says to Evie. "You're inquisitive like yer father and yer grandfather before yer." Evie loves hearing this; it makes her feel fluttery inside.

But right now, she's desperate to tell Grandpa about the creature. She slips past Cook and races down the hallway in search of him.

Evie bursts into the study, dripping wet. She sometimes barges in without meaning to, catching Grandpa unaware. She finds him leaning against the mantlepiece of the fireplace and when he looks up, his face is full of sorrow. Every now and then she forgets Papa was his son and how much he adored Mama. The world turns a little darker and Evie goes to him, wrapping her arms around his neck. She squeezes tight, until the sadness goes away.

"You've been on such a long walk this morning. I was beginning to worry," says Grandpa, dashing tears from his cheeks and plastering a smile on his face.

The study is their haven. It's lined with floor-to-ceiling shelves filled with leather-bound books, academic papers and taxidermy bird specimens. The mantelpiece is full of treasures Evie's found on her beach walks – feathers and shells, sea urchins and cuttlefish, sea sponges, and driftwood.

Grandpa was once a famed ornithologist and although he hasn't written a scientific paper for a long time, he's published hundreds on native, sea and freshwater birds.

The bookshelves also contain live specimens. Claudette, a lithe ginger cat, loves heights and sleeps on the fifth shelf, curled up on a crochet blanket. And Florette, a petite tabby, prefers the cane basket lined with wool on the bottom shelf. They adore this cosy room as much as Grandpa and Evie. When the weather is bleak, the cats don't leave the shelves.

Evie hops from one foot to another.

"What treasures have you found for me today, Evie? I can see you're excited," says Grandpa.

Cook marches into the study, muttering and cursing as she hands a bath towel to Grandpa. She's come to expect that when Evie returns from her walks, she'll be wet or muddy, or both.

Evie hurries to the bookshelf and runs her fingers along their cool spines.

"What are you looking for? *The Birds of Australia*?"

The Birds of Australia is Evie's favourite book in the whole, entire world. It has an illustration for each bird and lists their scientific and common names, as well as descriptions about habitat and even bird calls. Evie loves to listen out for birds and then guess what species they are.

Grandpa locates the book and gives it to her. She knows her powers of observation are excellent and he relies upon her keen eye to spot different species of birds his failing eyes can no longer see.

He cradles the book in his hands and stares at it with adoration, stroking the front cover. A flash of regret flickers across his face, but it's only brief. Evie knows Grandpa so well, but she's often confused by his reaction to it.

It's a mystery. One day I will find out what it is she thinks.

Grandpa holds the book out to Evie, but she shakes her head. It isn't the book she's after today. She pauses to tickle Florette under the chin before she spies the one she's looking for.

As Evie flicks through *Prehistoric Animals: Volume 1*, Grandpa towel-dries her hair. The book's spine creaks as she turns the pages. She soon spots the animal she's looking for and taps on a picture of a triceratops.

"Is that what you've found for me today? A dinosaur? Well, how wonderful."

Evie slams the book shut. She grabs Grandpa by the cuff of his tweed jacket and drags him towards the door. Laughing, he follows her outside.

"What have you found, Evie?" he asks under his breath, following her into the cool darkness of the stables.

CHAPTER 5

As Evie and Grandpa enter the dimness of the stables, Evie chews on her lip, suddenly uncertain about bringing the creature home. But it was injured and she feels Grandpa would have done the same thing, so she leads him by the hand to the foaling stall.

"Let's have a look at this mysterious dinosaur you've found me. Hold on now, Evie. I have to let my eyes adjust to the dark."

From the door of the stall Grandpa lowers his eyes to take in the sleeping mass on the straw. Evie watches him step closer, bending forward to get a better view. He rubs his eyes and takes another step, leaning in further still.

Grandpa's face contorts as he takes in the enormous size of the creature before him.

"Good gracious!"

Grandpa grapples with the stall door and, as the colour drains from his face, he promptly faints, crumpling onto the straw with a soft sigh.

Evie crouches down and fans her hands above his face. It dawns on her that she may not know what the creature is, but maybe Grandpa does. *It is dangerous!* thinks Evie, but she quickly calms herself, shaking her head. *No, this creature is nothing but kindness. I know it in my heart.*

Grandpa is moaning as he comes to. His brow is sweaty and his face is a queasy shade of green. He rises onto his elbows, and blinks a few times. Evie realises he's trying to remember what happened. When he does, he scrambles backwards.

"Evie! Quick, move away," says Grandpa, waving at her. "That is not a dinosaur. Do you know what it is?"

Evie shakes her head.

"I cannot believe I'm saying this. I must sound completely stark-raving mad. It's a rhinoceros, Evie. And they're very dangerous. Oh, my giddy godfather." Grandpa cradles his head into his hands. "Where did you find it, dear child?"

Evie points to the beach.

"You found it on the beach?" Grandpa's voice is high and thin and for a moment he's speechless.

"Does it have one horn or two?" he stammers.

Evie holds up one finger.

"All right, now, let me think. If it's only got one horn, it's an Indian rhinoceros. Now, from all accounts it's been hand-raised, probably as an orphan, so it's more than likely domesticated."

Grandpa paces the yard, his hands clasped together. "Is it a male?"

Evie nods.

"Oh, my. What do we do with it?! Is it injured?"

Evie mimes cuts on her arms and legs.

"I have to contact the authorities immediately and have it removed. You have to be terribly careful around him, Evie."

Evie gives a small smile. In the two years she's lived with Grandpa, he's marvelled at her understanding of animals, how quickly she gains their trust and befriends them. He even calls her the Pied Piper.

"All right, all right. I'm sure he's a kindly enough fellow. I know you're wonderful with animals, but you need to have your wits about you. I believe they have rather poor eyesight, so they can be unpredictable. Promise me you'll be careful?"

She nods her head again, crossing her heart.

"A rhinoceros?" Grandpa mutters under his breath. "An *Indian rhinoceros ... here?*"

CHAPTER 6

In the study, Grandpa paces up and down before slumping into his wing chair by the fire. Evie kneels at his feet nursing the *burk burking* Albine. She stares up at him, her eyes as large as dinner plates.

"It's all right, dear girl. I just need a moment."

The wind whistles around the chimneys of Lunar House. It's an eerie sound but Evie's lived here so long, she loves it. It means winter is coming. Last month, when the winter storms began, Grandpa boarded up all the upstairs windows. Yet they're still rattling and banging.

"Blast the south-easterlies," says Grandpa. "I hope that wind doesn't blow any more tiles off the roof. I have a list of repairs a mile long."

The colour returns to his face and he rubs the whiskers on his chin.

"Where on earth has it come from?"

Evie opens her mouth, but as usual nothing comes out. She's been like this since Mama and Papa's funeral, when she couldn't cry. It feels like something is wedged in her throat and every time she goes to say something it seizes. Grandpa tells her it's because of shock, that grief can sometimes do that to a person. He says her voice will eventually return and she mustn't worry about it. But at times like this, it would definitely make things easier if she could just use her words.

"Beyond the break, there's a shipping channel used by steamships coming from and going to Asia and England. I bet that's where it's come from. Did you see any signs of a shipwreck, Evie?"

Evie nods, her hair a tangled bird's nest.

"Lead the way," says Grandpa rising from his chair.

Down at the beach, Evie points out all the things washed in by the storm. They wade through floating wooden planks and ropes and barrels and bottles and hessian bags.

Grandpa doesn't say so, but Evie knows he's looking for survivors.

She wishes she could tell him she's already checked and it's as if he's read her mind when he says, "Don't worry, Evie. I'm sure the crew managed to get themselves into a lifeboat or clung to a piece of wreckage – the current would've brought them ashore. Come on, let's see what else has washed in."

They found nothing else of note, so Evie and Grandpa walk back to Lunar House.

"I need to find Mr Duffer so he can take me into Breamlea to report the shipwreck. But while he's getting the buggy ready, let's check on the rhinoceros," suggests Grandpa.

Mr Duffer, their farmhand, has worked for Grandpa for over thirty years. Evie can't recall a time he hasn't been there. He's quiet and amiable and knows a great deal about the farm and the weather. His eyes are always looking skyward, and in his attempts to predict rain, he lets Evie know about any birds he's spotted. She often meets him walking near the paddocks, checking on the cattle, patting their fat, glossy rumps and talking to them like children. Mr Duffer cares for Lunar House as if it were his own, and he and Grandpa discuss the farm and the weather for hours.

Near the stables, Grandpa and Evie find him repairing a fence. A gust of wind blows his tartan cap off and as he snatches it back he catches sight of them and gives a cheery wave.

"Mr Duffer, I need to go into Breamlea," says Grandpa.

"Are yer sure yer want to attempt it, Mr Strahan?" says Mr Duffer, looking up at grey stormy clouds.

"I understand, Mr Duffer, but unfortunately I need to send an urgent telegram."

Mr Duffer nods and heads off to catch Bernard the old coach horse and prepare the buggy.

At the stables Evie and Grandpa find Rhino sound asleep, snoring peacefully.

"It doesn't look like he's stirred much," says Grandpa.

The water bucket is empty and Evie refills it as Grandpa checks over Rhino.

"He's got a few cuts and scrapes, hasn't he?" he says, pointing at Rhino's legs, torso and flanks. "Evie, can you get your father's salve from the tack room?"

Evie's papa was a veterinarian and his pots of remedies still sit in neat rows on a shelf in the tack room, as if he's still here. She often went with him on his rounds to treat sick animals. She remembers watching him clean a leg wound of a prized breeding cow. She listened as he explained the importance of flushing it with clean water to remove all the dirt so infection didn't set in. He taught her how to apply bandages at just the right pressure for healing, how to suture without pulling the stitches too tight and the best way to drain an abscess.

Evie had seen Papa's affinity with animals. She'd studied his ways, noted his calm soothing voice and witnessed his steadiness. He always made eye contact with animals and was gentle and methodical in his treatment, always moving his hands slowly, never scaring them. Never rushing them.

"Let them sniff you," Papa always said to Evie. "It's an important part of any introduction. Blow in their nostrils so they can smell you, so they can see you. Show yourself, be open-hearted and they'll trust you."

Evie watched and listened.

"An animal will tell you what's wrong," Papa told her. "Watch their body language. A wide-eyed animal is alarmed. A fixed stare, a rigid stance, flattened ears, a frantic swishing tail, or repetitive licking are all telling us something."

Discomfort, nervousness, pain.

Evie watched and listened and learned. She is remembering everything Papa taught her and her stomach flips. Grandpa has said on more than one occasion, she has his gift, his affinity with animals.

She reaches for the special antiseptic ointment Papa made for healing wounds, a boiled mixture of melaleuca, calendula, pine and arnica, strained and mixed with bees' wax.

Twisting the lid off the jar, Evie inhales. His hands always smelled of this ointment. She closes her eyes and hugs the jar to her chest, waiting for the memories to shatter into sadness. She can remember his voice, his face, his laugh. How can a smell do that to you? Help you remember? Evie's mouth forms a wobbly smile. This is the first time it's felt good to think about him.

Rhino snuffles in his sleep. With the ladies perched above him, Evie and Grandpa smear salve on all his wounds. They remove several splinters with tweezers, and bathe encrusted salt from his eyes.

"That's about all we can do," says Grandpa, ruffling Evie's hair. "When he wakes up, mix him a bucket of bran and molasses, that'll get him as fit as a fiddle again. Be careful around him, Evie. As placid as Rhino appears, he's exhausted and in unfamiliar surroundings. It might take time for him to settle in. I'm off to Breamlea."

Evie nods and Albine *burk burks*. She knows Grandpa is concerned, but Rhino has shown nothing to be fearful of during his wakeful times.

The rain starts to tumble down and Evie sits in the straw next to Rhino, with Albine nestling in her lap, *burk burking*. The ladies roost in the beams above and Evie feels an odd sensation wash over her. She feels calm. Peaceful. She dwells on it, and recognises these feelings for what they are. She's happy.

Rhino wakes only the once, lifting his sleepy head to look around his stall. He feels confused, thinking he's still on the ship. But there's no swaying and rolling from side to side. He's lying on dry, sweet-smelling straw. He just feels so tired; every muscle in his body aches. But then he remembers, he can't be on the ship, it broke apart beneath his very feet and he swam ashore. He blinks and as he's trying to focus, a delightful aroma fills his nostrils. It's so familiar, it makes his heart squeeze. It reminds him of home and his throat aches. It's the dusty, earthy smell of feathers. A chicken appears before him. It's a very small one, and she's standing there making soft, welcoming sounds. Reassuring sounds.

Burk burk.

Rhino introduces himself by blowing air from his nostrils. The chicken is a tiny ball of black and white-speckled feathers. Two beady eyes stare up at him. He can tell she's brave by the way she stands with her shoulders back and her wings neatly tucked in. She eyes him off directly without flinching. Chickens can be like that. Rhino has met chickens like her before. She's a bossy one, but he immediately likes her and she pecks his horn.

Rhino realises his tongue is plastered onto the roof of his mouth; he's parched and desperate for a drink of water. And that's when he half sits up and sees her. The golden-haired child. He gazes at her and she him. The human child knows things, he senses. She too has seen suffering and he blinks both eyes at her. She disappears and he wants to bellow for her to come back but instead croaks like a frog. She returns as quick as the wind with a bucket of water and he drinks deeply. It's icy cold and delicious, tasting of minerals and green moss.

The human child disappears again, but this time Rhino doesn't panic. Somehow, he knows she will return. When she does, she feeds him something so delicious and delectable, his heart expands with his stomach. He can't help himself and gobbles it down quickly, licking the bucket clean. Fully sated, sleep calls him and his eyelids begin to droop.

Rhino knows the next time he wakes, the human child and the tiny chicken will be there and the little flickering light of hope inside of him grows.

Evie watches Rhino take in his surroundings. He seems dazed, but calm and accepting of his situation. He seems comfortable with Albine who won't leave him alone.

Rhino stares at Evie and blinks both eyes at once in acknowledgement. She's pleased he enjoyed the bran and molasses and she rubs his cheek and scratches his neck.

Burping loudly, Rhino slumps down into the straw, falling straight back to sleep.

Evie knows the fact he's eating and drinking is a good sign, but as she strokes his head and whispers into his hairy ear, Rhino begins a sleep that will last for three days and three nights.

CHAPTER 7

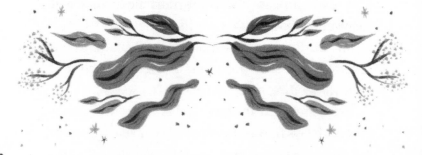

While Rhino sleeps, Evie hears the crunch of buggy wheels coming through the front gate of Lunar House.

A buggy ride into Breamlea usually takes about thirty minutes, but Grandpa and Mr Duffer have been gone most of the day trying to find a place to cross the creek. Bream Creek, a tributary of the Thompson River that flows through Breamlea village, is about two kilometres from Lunar House. Built on a rise, they're spared from seasonal flooding.

Evie places Albine in the straw next to the sleeping Rhino and hurries to the house to see how they got on.

In the kitchen everyone is talking all at once. When Grandpa sees Evie, he holds his arms open to her, enveloping her in a huge hug.

"We couldn't find a way through the flood waters, Evie. The banks of the Thompson have burst and the water is flowing fast. It's too dangerous."

Mr Duffer nods, despondent. "We attempted several creek crossings. Bream Creek is well and truly flooded. None of 'em is safe."

Evie's stomach flutters. The land around Lunar House always floods this time of year, leaving them cut off for weeks on end. *Rhino is going to be staying*, thinks Evie. *He's staying!* She wants to dance a jig, but Grandpa's face is downcast.

"Come on now, Mr Strahan and Evie, yer must be starvin, I have yer dinner 'ere waiting for yer," says Cook preparing to serve them in the study.

"Please, Cook. We're happy to eat in the kitchen with you and Mr Duffer. It's been quite a day," says Grandpa, rubbing his face with his hands.

Cook tut tuts. She disapproves of the master of the house eating with his staff, but she gives in, happy for the company.

Sitting down, Grandpa places his hands on the kitchen table and exhales.

"I guess now is as good a time as any," he says to Cook and Mr Duffer. "I'm not sure how to put this, but it might surprise you to know, there's a rhinoceros in the stable."

"A what...?" cries Cook.

"Did you say a *rhinoceros*?" Mr Duffer's cap falls off and he blinks several times as if he can't quite take in what Grandpa's said.

"Oh, Lord," puffs Cook, her cheeks reddening. Every part of her, including her apron, is trembling. She's trembling when they sit down to eat their shepherd's pie, and she's still trembling when Mr Duffer insists on making her a cup of tea after dinner.

"How on earth did it git 'ere?" asks Cook, stammering. "Don't they 'ave dangerous horns on their snouts or somethin?"

"Ah, yes. Yes, it has a horn. Quite a long one, actually."

Evie bounces up on her chair, holding her hands out wide to give Cook and Mr Duffer an idea of exactly how massive Rhino's horn is. But Grandpa gives Evie a quick shake of his head, gently pushing her hands down.

"Evie found it on the beach this morning," says Grandpa. "There's been a shipwreck. That's why I needed to go into Breamlea, to report it. The rhinoceros is injured and Evie put it in the foaling stall to recover."

"O' course, she did," sighs Cook, shaking her head. "Always bringin' this, that an' the other home, and God knows what else."

Evie slides from her chair and sidles over to Cook, placing her hand on her arm.

47

"Evie believes it to be good-natured, Cook. She is a reliable judge of animals. For all we know, it could be as domesticated as a cow," says Grandpa, shooting a glance at Evie.

Cook and Mr Duffer look at each other and nod in agreement. They've all witnessed Evie's kindness and patience with animals. The ladies, in particular, receive much attention from her, and they cluck around, happily laying eggs every day. Cook once witnessed Evie calm a distressed chicken. She held it like a baby and stroked its feathery chest until it stopped squirming. The chicken squarked and gave a soft sigh. Its wings drooped and its head flopped backwards. Cook believes Evie hypnotised it!

Both Florette and Claudette were feral kittens rescued and tamed by Evie and when Francie and Freddie first arrived, they were disobedient and uncontrollable. Now, they readily respond to hand commands to "stay", "sit", "come" and "go way back". Mr Duffer has also witnessed Evie's ability with their old coach horse Bernard. Ageing and cantankerous, he refused to be harnessed until Mr Duffer came across Evie blowing in his nostrils and staring into his eyes. From then on, Bernard worked steadily without a problem.

Cook's head jerks up as she pleads, "If I can't git along with the house cow, how will I manage with a bleedin' rhinoceros?"

"I'm as uneasy about this as you are, Cook. But with all the rain we've had, we have no choice. Rhino will be staying with us until the floodwaters recede."

Evie's heart is pounding and she smothers a smile. But it's too late. Grandpa sees it and he raises his eyebrows at her.

"Now, you listen here, my dear girl. Rhino is not yours to keep. As soon as we can cross the floodwaters we'll be reporting this shipwreck. The authorities will notify Rhino's rightful owners and they will come to get him."

"Aye, he's not a bleedin' pet, child," mumbles Cook, patting Evie's hand.

Thunder can be heard rumbling in the distance and heavy rain begins to hammer down.

"Surely, it can't rain for ever," says Grandpa.

Evie prays it does. She flexes her toes to let them know they're going to the stables in a minute to tell Rhino he's staying on with them.

"Everything will be all right," Grandpa promises them. "The chickens have taken a fancy to Rhino and I've always said chickens are a good judge of character."

"Chickens, pah!" says Cook, shaking her head. "It don't feel right, Mr Strahan. It shouldn't be 'ere, monstrous great thing. And yer say it has a horn!"

Grandpa nods. "I agree. It doesn't belong here."

CHAPTER 8

Three days later, Evie wakes to birdsong. She listens in the grey morning light and guesses by the high-pitched trill, it's a lark. She eases out of bed without disturbing the sleeping Claudette and Florette, carrying her shoes down the hallway so as not to wake Grandpa.

She sits on the kitchen step, pulling her boots on. The steps have been worn smooth over the years and, as Evie runs her palms over them, she wonders how many times her mama and papa would have stood here.

Claudette and Florette appear, yawning and meowing, weaving in and out of her legs. She pats their sleek bodies, from the tops of their heads down to the tips of their tails. They follow her as she heads off to do her chores.

Rhino doesn't stir when Evie enters the stables. He continues to snooze while she tops up his water bucket and carries over six bundles of lucerne from the feed room for him to have for breakfast. She nestles in the straw next to Rhino and her fingers move gently, scratching him behind his right ear. Rhino huffs and sighs in his sleep.

Evie jumps up and collects the eggs for Cook. The ladies now nest in the stables after laying their eggs everywhere throughout the straw. Evie prays she doesn't step on one. She holds a toasty, warm, speckled brown egg against her cheek and thinks of Mama and her warm hugs and an ache grabs her at the back of her throat. She still catches herself calling out for her or about to blurt out a question for Papa. But it's then she remembers, they're not here. They're gone. For ever.

Evie stares at Rhino snuffling in his sleep. Yes, Mama and Papa are gone, but she doesn't feel so alone now. In the last four days, Rhino has become the centre of her universe. And she, his. Evie has spent hours curled into the crook of his neck reading while he huffles in his sleep. Sometimes she just daydreams, staring into the rafters. But she's also jumped up for water whenever Rhino's smacked his lips together, and hay and bran and molasses when his tummy's rumbled. She's bathed his sore eyes and removed ticks and tickled his hairy ears. During this time, Evie's listened. She's opened her heart to Rhino. And he to her. And through eye contact and facial expressions, they communicate in a language that is not made of words. They feel each other's thoughts and feelings.

Kissing Rhino on the nose, Evie places the eggs in a basket. She leaves them in the pantry for Cook and, grabbing a pail, she walks to the house paddock in search of Dominique, their handsome Friesian. Her nature is indifferent, but on better acquaintance she's a likeable cow. When Cook tries to milk her Dominique slaps her in the face with her poo-covered tail, steps on her feet and knocks the milk bucket over. But Dominique lets Evie milk her.

It's raining again, but it's not wetting rain. Sparkling droplets sit on Evie's coat and her hair turns to frizz. She spots Dominique not far away, dozing under the overhang of a cypress tree.

Evie clicks her tongue to let her know she's coming. She approaches Dominique front-on so the cow can see her. She kneels down and stares into her big brown eyes. Dominique breathes her in and gives a long-winded, lazy moo. Evie scratches Dominique's back on her favourite itching spot. After ten minutes of divine itching, she turns her head towards the dairy. Evie walks on ahead as the cow plods along behind her.

Evie's calmness reassures Dominique. Her milk flows and fills the pail in no time.

Skimming the top of the milk, Evie scoops out a small bowl of cream for Claudette and Florette. They yowl with anticipation.

Evie lets Francie and Freddie out of their kennels, ruffling their ears before they bound off to the dairy to slobber up any spilt milk.

Back at the stables she leads Bernard out of the stable yard and into the paddocks to graze. She waits for him at the open gate and in passing he bows before her, lowering his head. Evie blows good morning softly into his nostrils and rubs his ears.

With all her chores done, she wanders back to the kitchen with the milk.

"Thank yer, child," says Cook as she bustles around and removes freshly baked loaves of bread from the oven. They smell delicious and Evie's stomach rumbles. She can't remember the last time she felt this hungry!

Sitting at the kitchen table with Albine *burk burking* in her lap, Evie sighs with a huff.

She's waiting for breakfast. She's waiting for Rhino to wake up. She's waiting for the rain to stop. She's waiting for Grandpa to report the shipwreck.

That's a lot of waiting for a girl – and waiting is not something Evie's very good at!

CHAPTER 9

For breakfast, Cook makes Evie her favourite eggs, "Dunkeld Eggs", according to an old Scottish family recipe. She tears a slice of bread into pieces, soaks it in a beaten egg then pan-fries it until it's golden brown. Evie devours it and she sees the look that passes between Grandpa and Cook. They've also noticed the return of her appetite. Cook often accuses Evie of eating like a bird. Well, she's not pecking at her food this morning!

As Evie spreads toast with apricot jam, a loud ruckus erupts outside. There's mooing and bellowing and calling out and carrying on.

"What on earth...?" Grandpa and Evie jump up from the kitchen table and hurry outside.

There in the garden are Rhino and Dominique. It's the first time Rhino has ventured out of the stables since his arrival.

At last. He's feeling better! thinks Evie.

Rhino and Dominique's meeting involves a great deal of sniffing, snuffling, circling and loud mooing.

Everyone at Lunar House hears the racket and runs to see what the commotion is. The ladies appear, squawking and squarking. Claudette and Florette are roused from their slumber in the study and arrive squinting in the morning light. And Francie and Freddie bound into the scene, barking and whining as they pace around Dominique and Rhino.

Evie can see Cook watching from a distance, her apron trembling.

"Oh, dear," Cook wails. "Look at that bleedin' horn."

"Will it harm the daft cow?" asks Mr Duffer, who appears with a pitchfork in hand.

Evie moves to Rhino's side, placing her hand on his neck.

"No. No. I don't think so," says Grandpa, standing close to Evie to show Cook and Mr Duffer there's nothing to fear.

"Bloomin' circus 'round 'ere," mutters Mr Duffer, retreating slowly from the garden and into the kitchen to make Cook a cup of tea.

Soon the noise and excitement reach fever pitch. Evie smothers a giggle. It's as if Rhino and Dominique are trying to "out moo" each other.

Evie and Grandpa watch in fascination as Rhino and Dominique weave around one another, nose to nose, in a strange dance. They trample through the garden, churning the lawn into mud. Finally, Dominique, who never moves quicker than a saunter, breaks into a gallop and bounds off into the house paddock with Rhino in hot pursuit.

"Well, I never." Grandpa dabs his forehead with his handkerchief. "If I didn't know better, Evie, I'd say it's love at first sight."

Evie and Grandpa grin at one another.

For the rest of the morning, Evie keeps an eye on Rhino and Dominique. They graze together like old friends, easy in each other's company. They touch noses and flare their nostrils, blowing air. Dominique snuffles Rhino's face and ears. She licks his eyes clean and Rhino stands still for her, his eyelids fluttering as he sways with the attention.

After a time, they meander across the paddock and soon arrive at a gate that leads down to the creek. Evie opens it and lets them idle through.

Quite suddenly, Rhino stops dead in his tracks. He lifts his head high and sniffs the breeze; his ears flicker and rotate and his tail spins in the air. Snorting, he inhales.

A soft, swirling breeze that tickles the hairs in his ears brings him a brackish whiff of stagnant flood-water with rotting reeds and bullrushes.

Memories from long ago wash over him. Fish-tainted green water, moss-covered rocks, loamy soil and silt. It's been so long since his last wallow. His skin tingles at the very thought and now that he thinks about it, he feels decidedly itchy. His body twitches at the delicious memory of the delightful foulness of cold, black, silky mud. His ears flicker; he can hear the tinkling flow of water, frogs croaking and beetles clicking. But it's the sweet stench of the decay of tidal marshes that gets to him. It's too much. It's irresistible, and with that Rhino bellows and tears off down the paddock towards the delectable, tantalising smells.

Evie and Dominique glance at each other and chase after him.

When he arrives at the creek, Rhino takes an almighty leap. He lands in the bog, burying himself with a loud squelching noise. He's covered in thick, black glossy mud. Evie can't see anything until he blinks, opening his little eyes. She laughs. He bounces around on all fours, splashing with his feet, stamping and sloshing. He turns back to curl his lip at Evie, and she can't stop grinning at his antics.

Rhino swims out to the depths of the creek where he completely submerges himself. He resurfaces, spraying water everywhere. He bellows and swims in a wide circle. Paddling back to them, he bellows again, as if he's inviting them into the water. Dominique inches forward, eager to go in but not quite brave enough.

Evie smiles. She now knows how Rhino survived the shipwreck – he's a fine swimmer.

CHAPTER 10

Three days later, Grandpa spots Evie and Rhino wandering in the garden and leaves the fuggy warmth of the study to join them.

Pale, puffy clouds sit high in the sky, but there's a sneaking streak of blue, with the promise of better weather.

"Rhino amazes me," Grandpa confides to Evie. "I can't recall ever seeing a more placid animal, let alone a rhinoceros."

Evie smiles and scratches behind Rhino's ear.

The ladies peck around him, weaving in and around his legs while he picks at the grass. Albine takes flight and sits upon Rhino's rump. He doesn't seem to mind, in fact, he doesn't bat an eyelid.

"I've always assumed the rhinoceros to be an aggressive animal. But upon further reading, I have come to the conclusion this is because people hunt them for their horns."

The word "hunt" sends a shiver through Evie. She too has been doing her own reading about the rhinoceros, discovering with disgust that their horns are a precious prize.

"This rhinoceros, however, has a genuinely kind soul."

As Evie picks mouthfuls of clover for Rhino, he's aware of her every move. It's like he has a sixth sense, always knowing where Evie is. She stops every few paces to pat his head and scratch his hairy ears.

In a cluster of foxgloves, a flittering sound draws their attention. It's a small bird, hovering as it drinks nectar from the bell-like purple flower.

Evie looks at Grandpa, her eyebrows shooting high.

"It's a spinebill, Evie. Not usually seen in these parts but, of course, unseasonal weather can change that. They're also called Tasmanian hummingbirds. See how it hovers to feed, rather than perch on a branch? They have a joyful way of floating through the air outside of time." Grandpa's voice sounds wistful. "Your grandmother Amelie believed when a hummingbird appears, anything is possible."

Smiling, Evie kneels down to watch the little bird. She leans back against Rhino and he snuffles her hair.

"Do you know why rhinos like mud, Evie?" asks Grandpa. He plonks himself down on the love seat in the rose arbour – or what *was* the rose arbour. It's now a tangled overgrown mess.

With her hand resting on Rhino's neck, Evie shakes her head and looks at Grandpa with inquisitive eyes.

"Rolling in mud keeps them cool. It removes parasites, like ticks, and it protects their skin, preventing them from getting sunburned."

A beam of winter sun peeks through the clouds. Evie holds her face up to it, enjoying the rays.

As she scratches Rhino under his chin, he snuffles her face and hair. He gently nibbles her ears, breathing in her milky honey scent. They're completely absorbed in one another and as they're gazing into each other's eyes, Rhino curls his lip and plants a soft kiss on Evie's forehead. It even makes a wet sucking noise. Evie wraps her arms around Rhino's head and they remain this way for the longest moment.

The golden-haired child is like the sun and the moon. He feels his heartbeat slow down at her touch when she scratches him behind his ears. The human child makes him see what's right in front of him. Strange hovering birds, juicy purple-coloured flowers, odd-looking trees he's never seen before. Silly, stupid dogs, who have actually turned out to be excellent company. Staring into her sky-blue eyes, Rhino sees himself, he sees where he's come from. He sees his memories, a window into his past and he can read her like wind swaying in the grass. His pain is still there; the blackness still lurks somewhere inside him. But she's a balm, like stinking black mud, only better. He feels her heart swell and he knows by the way her pupils dilate that she adores him. And the feeling is entirely mutual.

Grandpa sits up straight, bearing witness to this remarkable, tender moment. He rubs his eyes and leaves his hands clasped over his mouth.

"Oh, no. No, Evie. I have made a terrible mistake."

Evie looks at Grandpa in alarm. So too does Rhino, picking up on the change of tone in his voice.

"I should've sent Rhino away immediately," says Grandpa. "Blast the floodwaters. I should have done more, sent him somewhere, anywhere, as long as it was far away from here."

But Grandpa has always known that when Evie befriends an animal, she's devoted. She's just spent the past week caring for Rhino, spending every spare moment with him. They have bonded, like a limpet and a rock, and he knows their connection is pure-hearted.

Grandpa has just witnessed it with his very own eyes.

Evie knew the moment she locked eyes with Rhino there was something special about him, and it didn't take long for her to come to love him with the same fierceness she has for her own grandpa and for Cook and Mr Duffer and everybody else at Lunar House.

"How could I have let this happen?" whispers Grandpa. "How will I ever separate you two? Haven't you both been through enough?"

Evie goes to Grandpa and clambers up onto his lap. She wraps her arms around his neck and nestles her head into his chest.

Rhino plods closer and softly sighs. He hangs his head too, staring at them through long eyelashes, with a solemn expression on his face that says, yes, we are in agreeance. We have been through enough.

CHAPTER 11

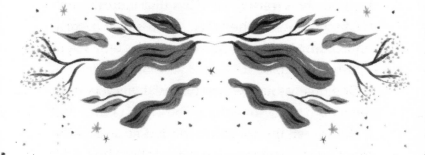

The next morning, Evie awakes to a shimmery pattern on her wall. The sun is pouring in through a gap in the lace curtains. She can hear the chirruping song of a blackbird and slips out of bed, leaving Claudette and Florette in tight, purring balls.

Hurrying into the kitchen, Evie bumps into Grandpa.

"Evie, the floodwaters passed their peak and have begun to recede. Mr Duffer and I are going to attempt to go into Breamlea. Would you like to come?" Evie bobs her head up and down.

"Go and get your coat then. And don't forget your bonnet and mittens," Grandpa calls after her as she races upstairs.

Breamlea, a small, pretty village, situated inland from the beach on Breams Creek, consists of a general store, a post office, a church and a boarding house. The streets are winding but orderly, are lined with moonah trees, with views that peek through to the beach and the creek. There's also a small school, which Evie used to attend.

When her parents died, Evie stopped going to school. She worried every time she went to open her mouth to say something, she'd start crying. And if she started crying, she might not ever stop. She might shatter into a million pieces. So Grandpa let her stay home and wander and walk and bird watch and collect treasure. But weeks away from school turned into months, and months turned into years. He always thought when Evie was stronger she'd want to go back. But she hadn't and Grandpa hadn't forced her.

The buggy ride into Breamlea is muddy but uneventful. When Evie and Grandpa arrive at the post office, Paddy Tait, the post office clerk, who also happens to be Cook's cousin, greets them warmly.

"Mr Strahan! Evie! Good morning to you both," says Paddy, shaking Grandpa's hand and winking at Evie.

"Good morning to you, Paddy. How are you?"

"Very well, thank you, Mr Strahan. And how is my dear cousin?"

Evie and Grandpa glance at each other. How is Cook? Her apron still trembles whenever she sees Rhino, but with Mr Duffer's help, she has managed to get close enough to peer at him from the stable door.

Grandpa coughs. "Cook is doing a fine job keeping us all in line."

"I don't doubt that." Paddy laughs. "Now, what can I do you for?"

"I need to send a telegram to the Maritime Board in Melbourne."

"Certainly, Mr Strahan. Come with me."

Paddy sits Grandpa down at a table with a pencil and a piece of paper. He taps his pencil on the notepad and stares at Evie and Paddy. She knows he wants to tell them something.

"I heard a rumour in my ornithological circles last year that the Royal Melbourne Zoo had started bringing in exotic animals from around the world to bolster flagging profits. I'm almost certain Rhino belongs to them."

Evie's eyes widen and she stands very still.

"It so happens I know the director of the zoo. His name is Douglas Henley. We were colleagues in the Ornithological Society of Victoria. I counted him as a friend." Grandpa waves his hand at Evie and Paddy. "This was a long time ago and I have no wish to renew my acquaintance with Henley. In fact, I'd prefer not to deal directly with the zoo."

Evie looks at Grandpa with curious eyes. Her mind is ticking over. *I know that name. Henley, where have I seen it before?*

"That's easy. Don't sign it," says Paddy, interrupting Evie's thoughts.

"What do you mean, Paddy?" asks Grandpa.

"If you wish to remain anonymous, you could sign the telegram off as the Master and esquire of Lunar House, care of the Breamlea Post Office."

A smile forms on Grandpa's lips. "Perfect. Do I have your confidence, Paddy?"

"Watertight, I am, Mr Strahan," says Paddy.

Grandpa bends his head and pens the words for his telegram.

POST OFFICE TELEGRAPHS, VICTORIA

NO PECUNIARY LIABILITY IS INCURRED BY THE CROWN, BY REASON
OF ANY DELAY, DEFAULT, OR OMISSION, IN RELATION TO ANY
TELEGRAPHIC MESSAGE SENT OR RECEIVED, OR OMITTED TO BE SENT
OR RECEIVED, IN VICTORIA

TO: Maritime Board of Melbourne

22nd July 1891

Address:

1 Shipwreck	2 south	3 west	4 coast
5 Breamlea	6 Beach.	7 Stop	8 Cargo
9 washed	10 ashore.	11 Stop	12 Rhinoceros
13 sighted.	14 Stop	15	16
17	18	19	20

From Master, Lunar House, C/- Post office Breamlea

Paddy sits down at the telegraph machine and demonstrates to Evie how it works.

"I press this key 'ere and use a tapping code to pass on letters that form words to the telegram operator in Melbourne. It's called Morse Code."

Evie thinks it sounds like cicadas in summer when they snap their wings together.

Grandpa appears by her side.

"The wonders of modern technology, eh, Evie? Much quicker than a letter."

"Ah, yes, but much shorter than a letter," says Paddy. "The key, Mr Strahan, is keeping it to the point."

Evie and Grandpa soon discover sending and receiving messages by telegram is a slow business. After three hours and three cups of tea, they manage to piece together a full account of the shipwreck from the Maritime Board of Melbourne.

The *SS Bancoora* was wrecked on 14 July. There was no loss of life. The captain and the crew washed up at Torquay, the next bay around from Breamlea. In its cargo of wheat, oats and tea, there was also a menagerie of exotic animals bound for the Royal Melbourne Zoo.

"I knew it!" says Grandpa, snapping his fingers.

The Maritime Board also sent through a detailed list of the cargo aboard the *SS Bancoora*. As they're reading through this list, Evie gasps in surprise.

On the list of exotic animals is a young elephant calf, a three-year-old Indian rhinoceros, six rhesus monkeys, two white cranes and six exotic green parrots.

Grandpa looks down at Evie. "You haven't seen any monkeys have you, Evie? Or any strange birds?"

Evie shakes her head but her finger hovers over the baby elephant. Her eyes prick with tears and her heart sinks inside of her.

"I know, dear girl. Fancy taking an elephant calf away from its mother."

"Come on," says Grandpa, and he steers Evie outside. They sit on the front steps of the post office, and a sliver of winter sun breaks through the clouds. Grandpa puts his arm around Evie's shoulders and she leans into him.

"You know you can't keep Rhino, don't you, Evie? He's worth a great deal of money to the Melbourne Zoo. They'll come for him as soon as they are able."

Evie pushes her face into Grandpa's jacket. She can smell bran and molasses and smoke and ink. All things safe. Grandpa tut tuts and rubs the small of her back.

It dawns on Evie that not everything is lost. She now knows rhinoceroses can actually swim very well. So, why can't elephants? If Rhino made it ashore during the shipwreck, perhaps the baby elephant did too? Maybe ... it's wandering around the sand dunes this very moment, lost and alone?

71

Evie squeezes her eyes tight.

And the monkeys and the birds – what if they made it ashore too? *I have to find them!* thinks Evie. *I have to!* She jumps up, and tugs on Grandpa's sleeve. They have to leave, but before they can, Paddy appears with another telegram.

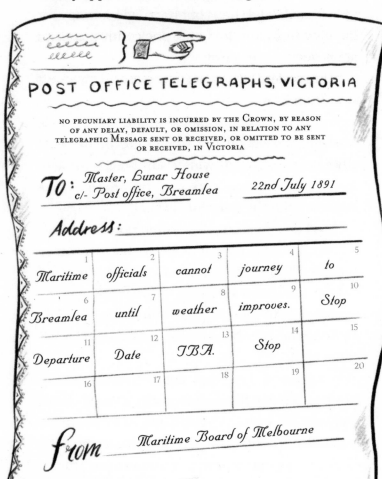

POST OFFICE TELEGRAPHS, VICTORIA

NO PECUNIARY LIABILITY IS INCURRED BY THE CROWN, BY REASON OF ANY DELAY, DEFAULT, OR OMISSION, IN RELATION TO ANY TELEGRAPHIC MESSAGE SENT OR RECEIVED, OR OMITTED TO BE SENT OR RECEIVED, IN VICTORIA

TO: Master, Lunar House
c/- Post office, Breamlea   22nd July 1891

Address:

1 Maritime	2 officials	3 cannot	4 journey	5 to
6 Breamlea	7 until	8 weather	9 improves.	10 Stop
11 Departure	12 Date	13 TBA.	14 Stop	15
16	17	18	19	20

from Maritime Board of Melbourne

"Thanks for your help, Paddy," says Grandpa, waving farewell as Evie drags on his arm, leading him towards Mr Duffer and the buggy.

Grandpa breathes a sigh of relief. "Well, we've done our duty, Evie. It's up to the Maritime Board to do their bit now and for the zoo to come and get Rhino," says Grandpa, with Evie beside him hopping from foot to foot as she continues to tug at his sleeve.

"Let's go, Mr Duffer. For some reason, Evie's keen to get home."

Yes, hurry! thinks Evie. Her mind is racing, whirring. *Where does one start to search for a baby elephant, monkeys and exotic birds?*

CHAPTER 12

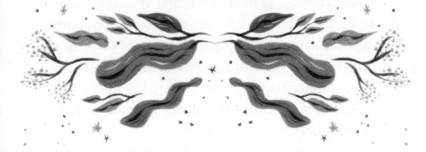

That night, Evie can't fall asleep. Her head is full of the baby elephant and her mind keeps tumbling the same questions over and over. What if it survived the shipwreck? What if it is hurt? Is it hiding in the bush? The very idea of it lost and alone in the bush makes her heart flutter. She snuggles into Claudette and Florette, but sleeps fitfully, dreaming of a baby elephant crying out for her in the night.

Evie awakes with a sense of urgency; all she can think about is where one might begin a search for a baby elephant, monkeys and birds. And if she is to find them, how can she show them she is friend, not foe? She knows the easiest way is to offer food. But what do baby elephants eat? She assumes milk, but will cow's milk be a good substitute? How is she to carry it? She's already researched a monkey's diet – fruit, nuts and seeds – which could also feed the birds.

With her head full of plans, Evie leaps out of bed and accidentally tips Claudette and Florette onto the floor. Dazed and blinking with sleep, they're far from impressed. She nuzzles them as she lifts them back onto the bed and nestles them into the quilt.

Evie dresses and hurries to her chores. She wants to keep some milk aside for the baby elephant and seems to recall a canvas water bag hanging off the side of the buggy. Perfect. She'll borrow that! Mr Duffer won't mind.

Downstairs in the kitchen, she catches a whiff of sweet pastry and the tang of apples. Cook has been baking, and there on a cooling rack in the pantry, are four golden-looking apple pies. Without a second thought, Evie wraps one in a tea towel and eases it into her shoulder bag. She adds three more apples, rhubarb stalks and a handful of oats. She can't believe what she's done – she's stolen an apple pie! But desperate times call for desperate measures. Even so, when Cook finds out, she'll string her up.

Evie hurries to the house paddock looking for Rhino. She finds him with Dominique and Bernard, and the sight of the three friends grazing together cheers her. They lift their heads upon seeing Evie and moo and neigh, calling out to her in greeting.

Rhino huffs as he saunters towards Evie making funny squeaking sounds as he snuffles her face. She rubs his ears and scratches his chin before tapping his horn and leading him to a fence. She steps up onto a railing and clicks her tongue, asking Rhino to move closer to her. He stands very still.

How hard can it be to ride a rhinoceros? wonders Evie.

Evie hoists herself up and climbs onto Rhino's back. With a squeeze of her legs, Rhino starts to walk. His gait is smooth and slow, much smoother than a pony's. Evie places her hands on Rhino's neck, and touches him on the left or right to show him which way she'd like to go.

It's not that different to riding a horse! thinks Evie. Except, you're a lot higher off the ground, and Rhino's girth is so wide her legs stick straight out. Evie grins. They head towards the beach to commence their search in earnest for the baby elephant, the monkeys and the birds. Evie feels hope floating around inside her.

Dismounting at the dunes, Evie and Rhino make the slow climb. At the top, the south-easterly wind whips at her hair and clothes. She inhales the clean salty air and juggling the shoulder bag, she staggers down to the bottom and onto the beach.

Rhino nibbles at Evie's arm, tugging at the bag straps. She loops the straps over his horn until it's secure and he carries the bag for her.

Together, these intrepid explorers stride up the beach.

We're going to find the baby elephant! We're going to find the monkeys! We're going to find the birds!

Evie smiles at Rhino's bouncy trot and his wobbly bottom. How she adores him!

Together they head towards the place Evie found Rhino and begin their search.

✦

The small cove is sheltered by a break of basalt rocks, and the aquamarine water is calm and clear. Evie glances at Rhino, wondering if he has any memory of this place. If he does, he doesn't show it.

Evie takes the shoulder bag from Rhino and together they meander up the gentle rise from the shoreline and into the marram grass-covered dunes. The dunes aren't steep here, they're more like rolling sandhills merging into tea tree scrub and bush.

Crouching down on her heels, Evie listens to the dunes with her hands. Rhino lowers his head and huffs down her neck. She runs her hands along the sandy corrugates and can feel the dunes vibrating. They're alive with bees buzzing in purple pig face and beetles and spiders making homes for their larvae, building nests and weaving webs.

What else can I hear? Evie concentrates, closing her eyes and going deeper.

Rhino closes his eyes too. He can smell something tangy, a nostril-burning smell. He knows it comes from the leaves of the trees in this area because he's chewed on some before, and they are most unpleasant. Very unpleasant. And this is a surprise, as his constitution allows him to consume most things. The dappled light through the trees makes him sleepy and he sways and leans his head lightly against the shoulder of the golden-haired child. She places her hand on his nose and "shushes" him. She wants him to be quiet. He can do that. He'll just have a little nap. But the human child appears to be searching for something. He can sense her alertness; her pulse is racing. Although, this isn't unusual. She is rarely still. Rhino gets a whiff of something on the breeze and it's the sweet, gagging rankness of over-ripe fruit. It's distinct and familiar. How could he ever forget it after the journey they endured together. He knows then and there, it's the reeking stench of the little monkeys. He has wondered what became of them after seeing them streak off into the sand dunes as he collapsed ashore. It dawns on him; this is what the golden-haired child is seeking. The monkeys.

Rhino jerks his head in the air and Evie's eyes fly open. She stares at him. His ears swivel and flicker. She knows he has an excellent sense of smell and acute hearing. She watches him as he tilts his head, sniffing the breeze. The pungent stink of monkey armpit wafts over him again. They're close, Rhino can sense it. He can hear the creak of branches, bending under the weight of something swinging from it. He has to let them know they'll be safe with the golden-haired child. The little monkeys were terrified of the humans on the ship, but they don't need to be with this tiny human. She is uncommonly monkey-like herself. Rhino bellows, calling to them. Reassuring them. He can hear their chitter chatter of nervous surprise. But he can also hear their uncertainty.

Evie cocks her head. She too can hear something. It's faint, but getting louder, clearer. Is it a bird? No. It's a chattering sound. Evie sucks in her breath. She imagines it's the sort of sound a monkey would make. *Monkeys*, she thinks, her heart fluttering. *It's monkeys!*

The wind gusts and as it changes direction the chattering fades.

Evie and Rhino move forward with deliberate,

slow, silent steps into the tea tree scrub. Evie scans the ground looking for any signs that animals have been moving through the undergrowth. Papa taught her how to track, to search for signs such as footprints, trampled grass and droppings. A hush falls around them and Evie raises her hand signalling Rhino to stop.

He's picked up all of the signals she taught Francie and Freddie. Rhino does stop, and from behind gently bumps into her. He nibbles her fingers as she stares into the bush holding her breath. A flash in the corner of her eye makes her head spin around, but there's nothing there. Another flicker of movement catches her eye and she snaps her head the other way.

There's something in the trees, or is she imagining it?! No! There *is* something in the trees, something *swinging* from branch to branch!

Evie and Rhino continue to stare into the bush. There is definitely something in the trees watching them. Rhino sways on his feet from side to side.

Taking the bag from her shoulder, Evie leaves their food offerings on the ground. She pours some milk into an old cracked ceramic bowl she found in the stables and leaves apples, rhubarb stalks, a pile of oats and, finally, she places Cook's apple pie on the ground. It's a bit mushed up. The outer edges are crumbled and merged into the sticky sweetness of the golden apples.

Evie's not sure how she'll cover up the disappearance of the pie, but she can't think about that right now. She has to focus on finding the baby elephant, the monkeys and the birds.

They leave the food and reverse out of the bush, back through the dunes and the swaying grass down to the beach.

Tomorrow, Evie and Rhino will return to see what is left.

But Rhino is reluctant to turn for home. He keeps stopping and turning his head around, staring wistfully towards the bush. He dawdles, dragging his feet in the sand, but after a while he canters to catch up with the golden-haired child.

CHAPTER 13

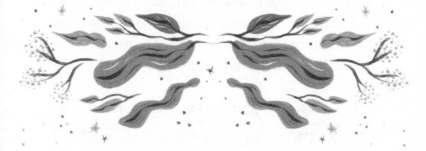

In the afternoon, squally wind and rain set in and Evie and Grandpa bunker down in the study. Claudette and Florette are on a warm rug in front of the fire, curled up like croissants. Rhino is snoozing in the stables with Dominique and the ladies.

Grandpa sits by the fire in his wing chair reading, and Evie sits opposite, reading with Albine *burk burking* in her lap. Evie has a selection of books to read about elephants, monkeys and exotic birds as well as a book about zoos, featuring the London Zoo, the Paris Zoo and the famous Berlin Zoo.

Having never visited a zoo before, Evie begins this one first. She's reading it with relish until she stumbles upon some disturbing illustrations.

Large species in tiny spaces, night enclosures without windows. Evie shudders at a picture of an elephant with its feet chained to a floor. Tears pour from the elephant's eyes and it has a woeful, heartbroken expression on its face.

Evie shuts the book quickly and an old newspaper article, brown and discoloured with age, flutters into her lap.

ACCLIMATISATION SOCIETY OF VICTORIA REFORMS AS ZOO
5th April 1868

The board of the Acclimatisation Society believe a change of direction is required and is reforming as the Royal Melbourne Zoological Society. Board member, Mr Douglas Henley, will be taking over as director of the zoo. Long-serving fellow board member and famed Ornithologist, Mr Charles Strahan, has resigned from his post.

"I disagree with the direction of the board," stated Mr Strahan. "Acclimatisation is the introduction of animals to Australia that suit our climate and conditions, and it is meant to benefit all agricultural endeavours. I detest the idea of a commercial zoo. Sourcing and exhibiting animals not native to Australia is cruel and, frankly, a complete waste of money. It's a scientific fact, exotic animals die prematurely away from their natural habitat. Zoos with inappropriate enclosures with poor ventilation and insulation, combined with poor quality food will result in their eventual demise."

Evie shows the clipping to Grandpa.

"Oh, where did you find that, dear child?" Grandpa gives a sad smile, staring at the article. "Your grandmother, Amelie, always put little notes and newspaper clippings, pressed flowers and feathers at the backs of books. I think it's her way of letting me know she's still here, eh? She was proud of the stand I took." He gazes at Evie, his eyes full of love. "It's no secret how I feel about zoos, Evie. But this article was written years ago. I'm sure they are much better places now."

Grandpa laughs as Evie crosses her arms.

"Evie," he shakes his head at her. "I'm sure zoos have improved. Not before their time, mind you. When I was a part of it, the society always lacked in its scientific approach. I'll never forget when they wanted to introduce foreign flora and fauna to Australia. Would you believe they didn't like the songs of native birds?"

Evie raises her eyebrows.

"I know. In the 1860s, they imported birds from England, releasing thousands of them in Australia.

There were thrushes, blackbirds, starlings and sparrows. And in 1861, sparrows destroyed Australia's entire fruit harvest. It had a disastrous effect on the breeding of native Australian birds. Their nests were raided and their breeding grounds were taken over by introduced birds. I warned the society sparrows were vermin, but they didn't listen."

Grandpa sounds weary. He removes his glasses and rubs the bridge of his nose.

Evie's heart lurches at the thought of Rhino going to such a place. Images flash before her of him in a cramped cage, with little sunlight and fresh air and no green grass to nibble on. She feels quite unwell when Cook knocks on the study door.

"Sorry to interrupt yer, Mr Strahan, but Paddy's brought a telegram for yer."

Evie's heart gives a loud thud.

"Thank you, Cook."

Cook passes the telegram to Grandpa, but remains hovering in the doorway. "And I, er, don't mean to bother yer, but I'm an apple pie short."

"What's that, Cook?"

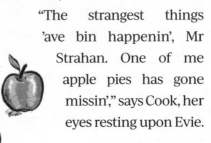

"The strangest things 'ave bin happenin', Mr Strahan. One of me apple pies has gone missin'," says Cook, her eyes resting upon Evie.

"I'm sure there's an explanation, Cook," laughs Grandpa, casting his eye over the telegram. "The pies can't just disappear into thin air."

Evie avoids Cook's steely gaze, stroking Albine's red comb as she watches Grandpa scribble a reply for Paddy to take back and send. *Oh, yes, apple pies can just disappear*, thinks Evie, feeling guilty.

POST OFFICE TELEGRAPHS, VICTORIA

NO PECUNIARY LIABILITY IS INCURRED BY THE CROWN, BY REASON OF ANY DELAY, DEFAULT, OR OMISSION, IN RELATION TO ANY TELEGRAPHIC MESSAGE SENT OR RECEIVED, OR OMITTED TO BE SENT OR RECEIVED, IN VICTORIA

TO: *Lunar House*
C/- *Breamlea Post Office*   23rd July 1891

Address:

1 Zoo	2 representative	3 coming	4 forthwith.	5 Stop
6 Have	7 you	8 seen	9 elephant,	10 monkeys
11 or	12 exotic	13 birds?	14 Stop	15
16	17	18	19	20

From   *Director Royal Melbourne Zoo,*
Sir Douglas Henley

If a hole in the ground opened up before her right now, she would happily be swallowed by it.

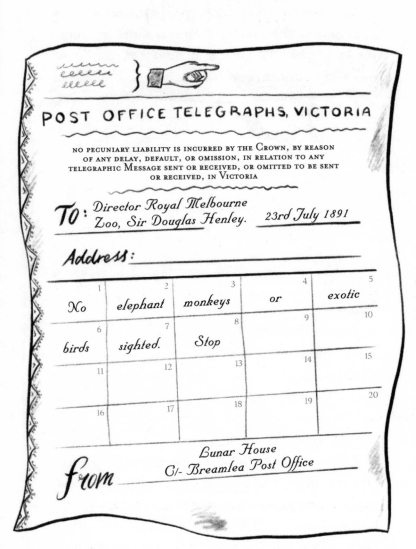

POST OFFICE TELEGRAPHS, VICTORIA

NO PECUNIARY LIABILITY IS INCURRED BY THE CROWN, BY REASON OF ANY DELAY, DEFAULT, OR OMISSION, IN RELATION TO ANY TELEGRAPHIC MESSAGE SENT OR RECEIVED, OR OMITTED TO BE SENT OR RECEIVED, IN VICTORIA

TO: Director Royal Melbourne Zoo, Sir Douglas Henley.   23rd July 1891

Address:

1 No	2 elephant	3 monkeys	4 or	5 exotic
6 birds	7 sighted.	8 Stop	9	10
11	12	13	14	15
16	17	18	19	20

from   Lunar House
C/- Breamlea Post Office

CHAPTER 14

The next morning, Evie and Rhino venture into the bush early to see what's happened to their food offerings.

Where are they?! wonders Evie with delight.

The apple pie is gone, except for a few pastry crumbs scattered about the ground. The milk has been consumed with little spillage and there are a few stringy bits of the rhubarb stalks and a sprinkling of oats remaining.

Evie and Rhino stand completely still, looking and listening. The bush sparkles with shafts of sunlight and the smell of melaleuca oil is strong. All is quiet, but Evie feels the hairs at the back of her neck prickle. She scans the trees and the strangest feeling washes all over her. She's almost certain someone or something is watching them.

Rhino moves closer to Evie until they're touching; she knows he senses it too. After wandering through the bush for about half a kilometre, Evie stops to place another offering of food on the ground. She couldn't bear to steal another one of Cook's apple pies, so she took six apples, a bunch of carrots and some sunflower seeds instead.

By leaving a trail of food for the baby elephant, the monkeys and the birds, Evie hopes to bring the animals closer to her. Closer to Lunar House. This is as far as her planning has gone though, and she'll work out what to do next when the time arrives.

When Evie and Rhino arrive back at the stables, they pass Cook. She's grumbling and complaining as she struggles to hang bed sheets up on the clothesline.

"My shoulders are killing me," says Cook.

Rhino saunters into the garden and Evie ducks into the kitchen. She's been avoiding Cook ever since the theft of the apple pie. From the window, she watches Rhino wander up to the clothesline.

Evie perches on the window seat in the kitchen to watch. As Rhino seems to be everywhere, Cook has forced herself to accept his presence, purely so she can get on with her chores. But she's seen how kindly he is with Evie and she's now brave enough to be in the garden with him. Although, she does carry a broom with her at all times.

As Cook turns to her washing basket to hoist up the next sheet, she jumps in fright at seeing Rhino standing there.

"Argh!" Cook trembles as she takes in the full size of him.

Enormous and magnificent, Evie sighs as she gazes out the window.

Cook's face pales and she squeezes her eyes shut, as if she's hoping Rhino might go away. Of course, he doesn't, and after a few moments she slowly opens one eye before seeing him and snapping it shut again.

Rhino is towering over Cook. He begins to sniffle and snuffle her neck and hair. Cook is quivering as Rhino knocks her bonnet off.

Just as Evie is about to go and rescue her, Cook's eyes flash open and they're full of fire. She puffs her chest out and points her finger at Rhino, wagging it at him, like she does to Evie when she's cross with her.

"I've never bin scared of anythin' in me life, an I'm certainly not going ter start now, no matter how big and ugly you are. So, go on with yer. Shoo!"

Rhino stares at Cook dreamy-eyed, chewing on his pink gums. He doesn't move, continuing to stand close by.

Cook huffs and shakes her head, deciding she's

just going to get on with the job of hanging the washing out.

Rhino watches her heave up another huge white sheet. He shuffles forward and nudges her hand. Leaning in with his horn, he hooks it into the corner of the sheet and raises his head, holding the sheet up for Cook to peg.

Cook gasps and pegs it onto the line.

As Cook reaches for the other end of the sheet, again struggling to lift it, Rhino steps in and holds it up for her while she pegs the other corner. They hang the washing out in no time.

"How did yer know how to do that?" Cook asks Rhino. She shakes her head and hoots with laughter. "Who would've thought I'd be talkin' to a rhinoceros? A bleedin' rhinoceros!"

Cook and Rhino gaze at one another for the longest moment. Then Rhino leans in and smacks a kiss on her cheek.

Cook gapes at him and touches her face where his warm rubbery, whiskery lips kissed her. She reaches up and strokes Rhino's nose. He snuffles her fingers and tenderly licks her hand.

She wanders back to the kitchen in a daze, turning every few steps to stare at Rhino and the sheets flapping on the clothesline.

Evie's heart sings inside of her. She's still gazing lovingly at Rhino through the window when Paddy Tait waltzes into the yard with his postal satchel slung over his shoulder. He glances around, looking to see who he might be able to deliver the post to.

Nearly toppling off the window seat, Evie knows this can only mean one thing – another telegram has arrived.

Evie trudges into the study.

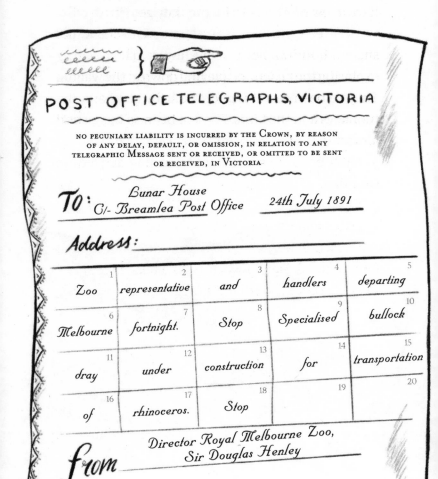

POST OFFICE TELEGRAPHS, VICTORIA

NO PECUNIARY LIABILITY IS INCURRED BY THE CROWN, BY REASON OF ANY DELAY, DEFAULT, OR OMISSION, IN RELATION TO ANY TELEGRAPHIC MESSAGE SENT OR RECEIVED, OR OMITTED TO BE SENT OR RECEIVED, IN VICTORIA

TO: Lunar House
C/- Breamlea Post Office   24th July 1891

Address:

1 Zoo	2 representative	3 and	4 handlers	5 departing
6 Melbourne	7 fortnight.	8 Stop	9 Specialised	10 bullock
11 dray	12 under	13 construction	14 for	15 transportation
16 of	17 rhinoceros.	18 Stop	19	20

From   Director Royal Melbourne Zoo,
Sir Douglas Henley

"Well, dear girl. We know this has been coming. The floodwaters are receding, but the roads are still muddy and rutted. It'll be a challenge for them to get that heavy bullock dray through. I'd say we'll have a few more weeks before they get here."

Evie feels unwell. For the past week-and-a-half she and Rhino have spent every day together exploring the beach and playing down at the wallow. They've been searching for the baby elephant, the monkeys and the birds. They've been so busy, she'd almost forgotten the zoo people were coming.

"It'll be a long and arduous journey," says Grandpa.

Evie holds her palms up at him in question.

"How many weeks? Who's to know, Evie?"

She wraps her arms around Grandpa and gives a long sigh. "All right, Evie. If I was a betting man, I'd say we've got a month until they arrive."

CHAPTER 15

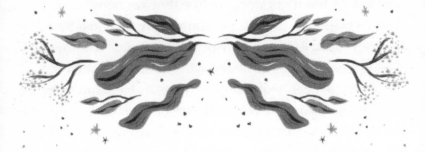

Evie dresses quickly in the chilly morning air. She moves swiftly through her chores so she and Rhino can continue their search for the baby elephant, the monkeys and the birds. They've checked the gardens, the sand dunes, the tea tree bushlands and eucalyptus groves down by the creek. She's decided they should go back into the tea tree bush as she was sure she sensed something was watching them in there.

Swinging past the pantry, Evie raids it of four pears, five blood plums and a handful of almonds. As she's about to leave, Cook and Grandpa arrive in the kitchen.

"There's strange happenin's around 'ere,

Mr Strahan," says Cook, gripping her apron.

Evie holds her breath.

"What do you mean, Cook?" says Grandpa.

"This mornin' another one of me apple pies disappeared. I blamed the child at first, but it can't be 'er, as I seen 'er doin' 'er chores."

Evie looks at the apple pies on the bench.

There's one, two, three ... oh, no! Where is the fourth pie? she wonders. Cook always bakes them in batches of four and there's only three! *What's going on?*

"That is strange, Cook," says Grandpa, sounding amused. "I'm not sure, but who would steal an apple pie?"

"Me thoughts exactly," says Cook with an exasperated sigh. "Me bloomin' ancestors were on the First Fleet for less. Stealing is stealing, it's just not on."

"I agree," says Grandpa. "I'll keep my eyes open, Cook."

Evie feels cornered; she doesn't want to be caught in the pantry by Cook, she'll get the blame. She sees the pantry window ajar and pushes it up. Easing her shoulder bag through, she clambers out over the sill and leaps, landing on the ground. She slides the window down from outside.

As she approaches the foaling stall, the ladies are *burk burking*, ready to go out for a peck. She can hear rustling straw, which means Rhino and Dominique are moving about their stall, also keen to go outside. Rhino huffles Evie's face good morning and she rubs his ears, leaning into him and breathing in his grassy smell.

She opens Bernard's stall and he shuffles out like an old man. He lowers his head for a pat before sauntering out of the stables after Rhino and Dominique.

On their previous search parties, Evie hasn't wanted to include Francie and Freddie. They're hunting dogs, but they're actually the world's worst hunting dogs as they're so playful. Previously, Evie thought their boisterous behaviour might be too much for a baby elephant, monkeys and parrots, and scare them off.

But now, Evie can see Francie and Freddie's exceptional sense of smell and tracking skills might be helpful. Time is running out. If the shipwrecked animals are still alive, they need to find them soon. They won't survive without help in the bush for too much longer.

Evie lets Francie and Freddie out of their kennels, and they bounce around her, eager for attention.

She slaps her hand on her leg, meaning she wants them to "come", which the dogs are more than happy to do.

Evie and Rhino wander along the beach in companionable silence. Rhino nudges her arm and she walks on with her hand on his shoulder.

Francie and Freddie follow them into the bush. They keep getting side-tracked as they find scents to sniff and seek, but Evie knows they'll catch up.

In the hope of drawing the animals closer to Lunar House, Evie leaves a trail of food. She plans to leave this morning's offering no less than eight hundred metres from the grounds of Lunar House.

CRACK! A branch snaps.

Evie and Rhino stop dead in their tracks. The sound is near. They look at each other, and turn their gazes back to the bush. Evie holds her breath. Her heart is thundering. She can't see anything. She listens for any noise that doesn't belong to the bush. But there's nothing. She stares at the ground, searching for footprints or droppings, but there's nothing. There are no signs of—

But there is! There, in front of Evie there are signs something has been curled in a clump of tussock grass. It looks flat and burrowed into, like a nest that something has tried to sleep in. That's what baby elephants do! They make nests in grass.

So do wombats, but Evie can't get the idea of it out of her head. She's not sure how big a baby elephant is, but it's possible, isn't it?

Francie and Freddie reappear, panting with their tongues hanging out.

Evie taps the ground with her hand, showing them where she wants them to get the scent. They sniff and snuffle in and around the tussock grass.

She waves her arm at them, pointing her index finger in the direction she wants them to go. With their snouts to the ground and tails aloft, they bound off into the bush.

As Evie sets out the food, goosebumps rise on her arms. She experiences the strangest, weirdest feelings.

Something is watching us. Rhino flicks and swivels his ears in agreement before they head off into the bush, trailing after Francie and Freddie.

Rhino plods after the golden-haired child. She knows. She knows the monkeys are here, somewhere. She has excellent instincts, for a human. The little monkeys are close by, but they're hiding. Monkeys are excellent at hiding and trickery. He huffs. They'll never show themselves to those silly, bouncing dogs. They're nervous, they can't yet trust anyone. But they may not have a choice. He can smell their rank armpit sweat, they're starving and exhausted in their attempts to survive. He has to let the monkeys know where the stables are, he can't stand the thought of them suffering. He stops and chews on his gums before tensing his flanks and holding his breath. He farts loudly. It's low and long and rumbling, almost tuneful, thinks Rhino, and it reverberates through the bush. There, that should do it. The human child giggles. He's not sure why she enjoys this natural function so much. But who is he to judge? Rhino passes some droppings and saunters after the golden-haired child and the dogs.

CHAPTER 16

Evie climbs up on a fence railing, clicking her tongue for Rhino to amble alongside. He understands and saunters over, standing still for her to clamber aboard. She settles and she clicks her tongue, squeezing her knees. They meander for miles through paddocks and marshes until they're down at the creek.

Evie thinks about the baby elephant, the monkeys and the birds, wondering if she's imagining hearing things out in the bush. But something is eating her offerings. Perhaps it's a wombat? No. Evie knows she has good instincts and Grandpa always tells her to trust them. She's looking forward to going back there tomorrow to check on them.

Rhino stops every now and then to tear at bullrushes and the tall stems of native yams.

Evie lies upon Rhino as he grazes, with her arms and legs trying to stretch around his massive girth. Daydreaming, she can feel his warmth, his steady heartbeat and the pops and squeaks of his inner workings. She can hear her own inner workings too. Dinner last night was so good. Evie couldn't stop herself from having two helpings.

When they reach the wallow, Rhino paws at the water. Evie slides off, knowing he wants to go in. She perches on a rock to watch him swim and roll around in the mud. He swings his head from side to side and swirls the water around with his horn. He stomps and splashes before lying down and sinking into the mud with a huff and a sigh.

After a while, Evie hears a strange noise. It's a bird, but it's an unfamiliar one, certainly not one she's ever heard before. Rhino hears it too. He sits up in the mud, his ears flicking and swivelling. Evie looks at him and shrugs her shoulders.

Then they hear it again.

Buzz buzz buzz buzz buzz.

It sounds like a cicada, but it isn't summer time.

Evie gets to her feet and signals to Rhino she wants him to "stay". She smiles to let him know everything is all right and walks to a nearby blackwood tree and cocks her head to one side.

There it is again!

Buzz buzz buzz buzz.

Scanning the branches, Evie spies two parrots high above in the canopy. The larger one is grass-green and yellow with an orange spot on his belly and a bright blue band across his beak. The other smaller bird is similar, but less colourful.

Evie's sure this parrot is special. She's never seen it before and it's particularly beautiful. She must tell Grandpa.

"Good afternoon, Evie," says Grandpa, sitting at his desk sketching. Although the drawing is upside down, Evie can tell it's of a Japanese snipe. She smiles and goes to the bookshelf to retrieve *The Birds of Australia*.

"Excellent," says Grandpa, seeing her choice. He pushes his drawing aside. "What have you found for me today?"

She places the book on his desk and flicks to the section on native parrots. Evie takes her time until she finds the exact bird. She circles it with her finger, making the paper hiss.

"No, Evie, the orange-bellied parrot? They're near extinct, my dear girl. The starlings ruined it for them when they were introduced to Australia.

They raided the nests while the parents were out feeding, destroying all the eggs. It was a disaster."

Evie wishes she could speak. It would make things so much easier, especially with this rare parrot she's found for Grandpa. She tries to form the word "Grandpa". She rolls it around on her tongue, she can hear and feel it, but it won't budge. She sighs, and taps the picture again, staring at Grandpa.

"It's all right, Evie. Tell me, it definitely has an orange dot on its belly?"

Evie nods.

"And it has a blue band between its eyes?"

Evie's head bobs up and down.

"Did it make a fast buzzing sound?"

Evie's eyes widen and she nods again.

"Good gracious. Can you remember where you saw it?"

CHAPTER 17

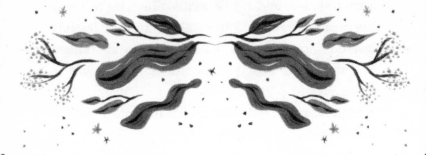

Grandpa rushes to saddle up Bernard.

"Do you want to ride with me, Evie?"

Evie shakes her head, climbing onto the fence. Rhino lumbers in beside her and she leaps onto his back, grinning at Grandpa.

He laughs. "Oh, Evie, you are sure to be a great explorer."

Away they gallop down to the creek, to the place Evie last saw the parrots.

While Bernard grazes on a loose rein with Rhino, Evie leads Grandpa through yellow wattle trees to a blackwood tree. But all is silent, and her heart sinks – they can't hear or see parrots anywhere.

"Don't worry, Evie. They'll show up. Remember,

we ornithologists need to be extremely patient." And with that, Grandpa whips off his coat, and spreads it on the ground for them to sit upon.

In the meantime, Rhino entertains Evie and Grandpa, playing in his mud wallow. He moos at them, splashes around, spurts water, floats and blows bubbles out of his nose.

Dominique appears and moos at the water's edge as if to say *How could you leave without me?* and Bernard paws the water with his hooves as if he too is keen to go for a swim.

Then Evie sees Rhino bob up. He's sitting very still, and staring off into the distance. He flaps his ears and Evie knows he can hear something they cannot. She hardly breathes, trying to listen. Then Rhino starts to swim towards them, staring at Evie.

Evie tugs Grandpa on the sleeve as Rhino staggers from the wallow. He comes to them and stands close, dripping with water, his ears flickering and swivelling.

Evie beckons Grandpa to stand.

"What is it, old chap?" Grandpa asks Rhino.

Rhino turns on his heel and with Bernard and Dominique in tow, they follow him along the edge of the creek.

At last, Rhino stops at a grove of eucalypts. He turns to stare at them and then tilts his head, peering high above to the top of a manna gumtree.

Evie and Grandpa scan its branches. And then they can hear it!

Buzz buzz buzz buzz.

Evie's eyes flash at Grandpa.

"By Jove, it's them," he whispers to her. He stares up at the trees, watching for movement and colour among the greenery. At last, they see a pair of orange-bellied parrots perched high above in the canopy.

"There they are!" says Grandpa.

Evie watches as he whips out his notebook and draws a map of their location. He jots down some notes and starts sketching the parrots. He pauses and rummages around in his pocket before passing a spare notebook to Evie, so she too can sketch them.

"But where are my manners?" says Grandpa. He slips his notebook back into his pocket and strolls over to Rhino, who is grazing with Dominique and Bernard.

"I can't thank you enough, Rhino," says Grandpa and Rhino curls his lip and leans forward, giving him a wet peck on the cheek. It's warm and prickly and Grandpa jerks back, touching his cheek.

"Did he just kiss me?" Grandpa laughs. "Rhino, you really do take the cake."

Evie smiles.

"You know what, Evie? It's been a long time, but I have a sudden urge to write another paper. I don't

Common name:
Orange-bellied
parrot

Scientific name:
Neophema chryogaster

Habitat:
Bream Creek,
eucalypt woodlands
Breeds: Nov - Dec.
Nests: tree hollows.
Size: 20-22 cm

know what's come over me, but I'm going to write about the near-extinct orange-bellied parrot!"

Evie savours Grandpa's laugh. She notices that his eyes are sparkling. She hugs him, realising it's the first time she's seen him this happy in a long, long time.

Rhino's heart lifts at hearing the golden-haired child and the old human laughing. He's never heard the old one make this sound before. It's wondrous. It's like the morning sun has arisen and it's warming him from the inside. He feels the air quivering, and he can't help huddling around them, crowding the two humans who care for him. It's a joyous feeling and he bellows so loudly, with such exertion, he accidentally farts. If he had known these two little twits in the trees would bring so much happiness, he would have brought them here earlier.

CHAPTER 18

With Albine *burk burking* under her arm, Evie waltzes into the kitchen with the eggs and milk and bumps into Grandpa and Cook.

"Evie, Mr Strahan. I need ter talk to yer both," says Cook, waving at them to sit down at the kitchen table. She has a serious expression on her face.

Evie raises an eyebrow at Grandpa and he shrugs his shoulders.

"Another one of me apple pies disappeared this mornin'. That makes three thefts! I'm sorry I blamed yer at first, child. I bin keepin' a close eye out fer who be doin it."

Grandpa puts his hand over his mouth, trying not to laugh.

Evie shakes her head.

Who is doing this? wonders Evie. Her heart skips a beat as she recalls the remains of the apple pie in the bush. *Would it be too much to hope that a little monkey has taken the pies?* She closes her eyes, wishing with all her heart this is true.

"Come an' ave a look at this then," says Cook.

Evie and Grandpa follow Cook into the pantry.

"In the mornins, I always open the window to let a bit o' fresh air in. But I must 'ave forgotten about it and another left it open ov'night. For I come in this mornin' and discover another one of me pies is missin'. But I see this – evidence of the culprit!" says Cook, puffing her chest out and pointing.

Evie is aware Cook sprinkles sugar on top of her apple pies as they cool. A layer of sugar covers the bench, except for where the missing apple pie had been. In this dusting of sugar, are the smallest footprints Evie has ever seen.

She sucks her cheeks in. *Monkeys! It's true! A monkey has been taking the apple pies. They survived the shipwreck!*

Evie follows the trail of white, sugary footprints from the bench to the windowsill outside. She can't be sure, but by the number of footprints she thinks there could be more than one monkey at play here. She stares closely at one of the pies only to see tiny holes in the pastry. Little holes made by little fingers! Little fingers that poked through the pastry to the delicious apple filling. Little hungry fingers, hurriedly licked before escaping with a pie in hand.

This is amazing! Evie's heart soars. *The monkeys are alive!*

Grandpa looks confused and glances from Evie to Cook, trying to understand.

"What exactly is going on here?" says Grandpa. "What are these footprints? Who's been taking the apple pies?"

Oh, no, thinks Evie. *Cook knows. She must have seen one of the monkeys. Please don't say anything, Cook. Please.*

Cook takes a deep breath and locks eyes with Evie.

Please don't say anything. Evie's eyes plead with Cook.

Evie really doesn't want Grandpa to know about the monkeys. He's as honest as the day is long and he'll tell the zoo and they'll take them, as well as Rhino, away for a miserable life in captivity.

Cook gives her a reassuring look.

Evie holds her breath.

"Bleedin' possums," Cook announces. "They're the bleedin' thieves."

"What? Possums wouldn't bother climbing in here for apple pies," says Grandpa. "They've got a whole farm out there to forage and raid."

"Oh, my word. Apple pies is a delicacy to 'em. They used to eat me mother's apple pies and me grandmother's before me," says Cook, nodding her head with an air of authority, that, yes, indeed she's seen this sort of behaviour before.

"Good Lord," says Grandpa. "Well, I never. Mystery solved." And he steps forward and slams the window shut. "There."

"Thank you, Mr Strahan," says Cook and she smiles at Evie. Her face is shining with light and as Grandpa exits the pantry, Cook winks at her.

Wandering back to the kitchen, Evie decides she likes it when Cook smiles.

CHAPTER 19

Evie grins to herself, recalling Cook's fanciful story about apple pie-eating possums. Why would Cook want to protect the monkeys? Is she also unsure about Rhino going to the zoo?

Evie has watched Cook and Rhino in the garden together. He always appears when she's hanging out washing and Cook chats to him as they work, always patting him on the nose when they're done. He saunters after her into the vegetable garden and she feeds him handfuls of freshly picked herbs and potatoes. He's also become quite partial to turnips. If Rhino even thinks about nibbling at anything else, Cook wags her finger at him.

Evie heads outside in search of the monkeys.

With Albine, her trusty partner trotting behind her, they commence their investigation.

A bough of a wattle tree is brushing against the house, near the pantry window. Evie's sure a nimble monkey could climb it and shimmy along a branch to the open window.

Peering out the window, Evie traces the sugary trail from the sill to the branch, to a fork in the tree and down the trunk. At the bottom, there are pastry crumbs! They must have dropped the pie when they leaped down from the tree. She follows the sugary crumbly trail with her heart high in her chest.

Albine *burk burks* as they follow the clues through the garden. Unfortunately, she begins pecking at the pastry crumbs and Evie has to carry her to stop her from eating the trail.

Albine *burk burks* her innocence as they push their way between gaps in bushes and hidden holes in hedges. The sugary crumbly trail winds and weaves, veering close to the house, hugging the walls. Evie and Albine follow the trail into the yard, and then it's gone! They've lost it! She huffs a frustrated sigh and walks back and forth across the yard looking for the crumbs. She's concentrating, with her head down, her blonde hair falling across her face.

"What are you doin', Evie?" says Mr Duffer, passing through the yard. He removes his tartan cap. "Have you lost somethin', lass? Do yer need a hand?"

For a moment, Evie's stumped for an answer. She shakes her head and points to a trail of ants, crouching down to study them. It's a weak cover story and Evie knows it. But being Grandpa's farmhand for so long, Mr Duffer's seen it all before.

"Alrighty." Mr Duffer looks at her, nodding, and continues on his way.

As Evie stares at the ants, something crystalline sparkles – sugar! And pastry crumbs! They've found the trail again, which zigzags across the yard towards the stables.

At the stable door, Evie glances around to make sure no one is about. Then she slips into the quiet dimness inside.

Breathing through her mouth, Evie's heart bangs against her ribs. Rhino and Dominique and Bernard are out grazing, and the ladies are outside too. There are no animals in the stables. Well, there shouldn't be, but there's definitely something in here. Evie can sense it. She moves silently. She can hear rustling!

Burk burk.

It's too late now for Evie to have second thoughts about bringing her sidekick with her. She strokes Albine's chest, softly blowing in her ear to quieten her.

Rustle rustle...

Evie freezes. *Where is that sound coming from?* The rustling takes her gaze high into the roof, into the hayloft. Movement!

Rustle rustle...

The monkeys are in the hayloft!

What can I do to help them? They have food in their bellies, apple pies to be precise, but Evie wonders if they are warm enough? *Is this why they're in the hayloft?*

Evie knows these rhesus monkeys are from India and used to a tropical, warmer climate. She grabs a horse rug – waterproof and lined with thick wool – from the tack room.

Up the ladder, leading to the loft, Evie carries the rug.

Rustle rustle...

As Evie climbs the ladder slowly, each rung creaks and squeaks.

Rustle rustle...

When Evie reaches the top, she places the rug on the hay.

She's desperate not to scare the little monkeys. From somewhere deep inside her, she begins to tremble. Her throat quavers as vocal cords stretch and pop and just as she thinks it might hurt, she feels a lightness as a strange sound resonates from inside of her. Evie begins to hum the soft lullaby Mama used to sing to her.

My voice! I can feel it! It's there, somewhere.

Evie's voice feels shaky and quavery and weak, but strangely reassuring at the same time. She realises the loss of Mama and Papa doesn't hurt quite as much as it used to, that since the shipwreck and the arrival of Rhino, she's been slowly waking up. She can feel an awakening in her heart.

Evie has to help these little monkeys, and she closes her eyes and sends them a message.

Do not be alarmed, little ones.

Rustle rustle...

The sound is coming from the far corner of the loft. Evie crawls on her hands and knees, continuing her humming. Parting the hay, she goes deeper and deeper into the loft, crawling on and on. At last, she pushes through the hay only to find two scared, little pink faces staring back at her. The monkeys are clinging to each other. They're shivering and they stare at her with fearful, hazel-brown eyes.

Evie sits back on her heels, still humming. She closes her eyes and sends them a message. *It's all right, little ones, it's all right. I'm going to look after you.* She opens her arms to them, like Grandpa does with her, and smiles at them, nodding her head as she hums.

And with that, the little monkeys leap straight into her arms. Evie can tell they're juveniles. They're small and lightly built, but one is noticeably smaller. Evie cuddles the little bodies to her. She rocks them back and forth, rubbing their backs and stroking

their little heads. They snuggle
into her and she can feel them
quivering. She can feel their bony
ribcages and can see they've got a few
cuts and bruises.

They're very friendly, which makes Evie wonder
if they had been hand-raised as babies, like Rhino.
They soon gain confidence in Evie and begin
chattering. In a rush, both chitter chatter at once,
as if they're telling her all about their journey and
their hardships. She holds them close, thinking
how brave they are.

Evie makes up a warm bed for them using the
horse rug. But the monkeys cling to her and won't
let her go, so she sits with them until they do. The
larger one is a male, and the smaller one is a female.
She places them inside the rug, as snug as bugs,

then hurries down the ladder to retrieve Papa's antiseptic remedy for their wounds.

The little girl doesn't flinch when Evie dabs the ointment on her cuts. But the larger boy, who has a crazy looking spiky hair-do, sucks the air in through his teeth as if it stings. Evie cuddles them both in apology until they settle.

Every time Evie gazes at the boy monkey, she can't help remembering her Great Uncle Simon. He had crazy-looking, spiky hair. Come to think of it, Aunt Minette, pink-faced and petite, was like the other little monkey. It's uncanny how much they resemble her old uncle and aunt.

It's a tad rude and disrespectful, but she names the monkeys after them anyway. *Sorry, Uncle Simon! Sorry, Aunt Minette!*

I hereby name you Simon, thinks Evie, as she tickles his tummy. Simon gives her a cheesy, gummy grin.

She touches the chest of the smaller monkey. *I hereby name you Minette. Mini for short. It really suits you, Mini*, and the little monkey chatters her teeth at her.

Evie cradles them softly, stroking their downy little heads, and thinks how beautiful they are. They sigh and snuggle up and they drift off to sleep.

With a full heart, Evie hurries to the house paddock in search of Rhino. He's grazing with

Dominique and Bernard and he lifts his head in greeting when he sees her and trots over.

Evie wraps her arms around Rhino's head and gives a little sob of relief. She's so grateful they've at least found two of the little monkeys. Sadly, there is no sign of the baby elephant or the exotic parrots, but she's doubly grateful for finding the dear little monkeys.

Rhino nuzzles her and it's then she notices a fine dusting of sugary pastry crumbs all over his head and ears, and Evie laughs and laughs until she hiccups.

CHAPTER 20

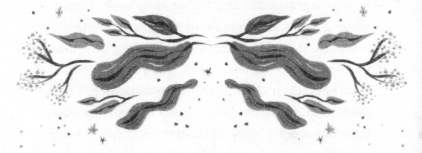

Evie hurries into the pantry only to find Cook has made a basket of food for the little monkeys. It's full of miniature-sized apple pies and rhubarb stalks and nuts and seeds. Evie picks up one of the mini apple pies, which fits perfectly into the palm of her hand.

Breathless, she dashes to the study to grab a book before racing back into the kitchen. She plonks it on the table and wraps her arms around Cook's waist.

"Did yer find 'em, child?" asks Cook, kissing the top of Evie's messy cloud-like hair.

Evie nods and waves two fingers at Cook.

"Two! I thought there might 'ave been two of

123

'em in me pantry. Poor little beggars, they looked pretty scrawny when I saw 'em. Scared the life outta me, and me outta them!"

Evie picks the book up from the table and opens it. It's Britannica's *World Encyclopedia of Animals* and she flicks to a page marked "Rhesus Monkeys" and holds it open to show Cook.

"'Tis them! Is that what they are? Ree-sus mon-kees. Dear little mites. Years ago, Evie, I had a wonderful ol' uncle who was a merchant sailor. Travelled the world, he did. Anyways, he 'ad himself a little monkey. Sweetest thing yer ever did see. I 'ave a real soft spot for 'em."

Evie closes the book and stares at Cook with wide, questioning eyes.

"Don't worry, Evie child, I'll not dob yer in. I've 'eard yer Grandpa talk enough 'bout them zoos and those poor animals livin' in captivity. I wouldn't wish for the little mites to live such a life," says Cook, smiling at her.

"Knock, knock," says Paddy.

Evie and Cook give a start, looking at each other in surprise. Neither of them heard Paddy arrive.

"Git on with yer now, child," says Cook.

"Mornin' to yer, cousin," says Paddy, walking into the kitchen.

"Mornin', Paddy," says Cook, glancing at Evie.

Evie knows Paddy's arrival only means one thing. She stands frozen, fixated on him.

"Got a letter for Mr Strahan. It looks important, so I thought I'd better bring it 'ere straight away," says Paddy, pointing to the gold crest.

"Oh, it is, Paddy," Cook tut tuts. "Mr Strahan has bin wonderin' on the zoo representative's whereabouts. Thank yer for bringing it." Cook puffs and pants as she bustles out of the kitchen in search of Grandpa.

Evie remains rooted to the spot, her eyes never leaving the letter in Paddy's hands.

Grandpa appears from the study and a look of worry passes between him and Cook, who is twisting her hands in her apron.

"Will yer stay for a cuppa, lad?" asks Cook.

"Thank yer, cousin, and I'd love a slice of yer apple pie?"

"Oh, I'm sorry, lad. We're a bit short on apple pie at the moment."

"Oh, it's not those possums again, is it?" says Grandpa, exasperated.

"No, no," says Cook. "I just need ter make more."

Grandpa beckons Evie into the study and she follows, her eyes downcast.

She stands with her back to the fire, watching Grandpa, her eyes too large for her face. Grandpa sits down at his desk and Albine perches quietly on her cushion in one of the wing chairs, watching on.

Grandpa opens the letter and reads aloud.

Dear Sir,

After several delays, due to difficulties in constructing a bullock dray designed to carry a rhinoceros, please be advised that on 2 September, a party of Zoo representatives will depart Melbourne to travel overland to the village of Breamlea to where the said rhinoceros from the fateful shipwreck of the steamship SS Bancoora was last sighted.

Leading this party is Mr George Henley, a Royal Melbourne Zoo representative. Weather permitting, the journey to Breamlea should take four days with an estimated arrival on 6 September. A team of expert large species animal handlers will be accompanying the zoo representative in a purpose-built bullock dray to ensure the immediate re-capture of the rhinoceros to secure its return journey back to Melbourne.

Yours sincerely,
Sir Douglas Henley
Director Royal Melbourne Zoo
Royal Park, Parkville, Victoria

Grandpa sighs and hands the letter to Evie to read.

"Look at the date, Evie. It's the twenty-sixth of August. Today is the second of September, so they won't be with us for another four days. Although pulling such a heavy dray through this weather will not be easy."

Evie feels the blood drain from her face. The room sways and she feels a swooping in her belly. She knew this was coming. But after nearly two months, it never felt like it would ever actually happen. It never felt real. Grandpa has told her over and over, she can't keep Rhino. She knows he doesn't belong to her, but she can't imagine life without him. A rising, aching blackness fills her. With trembling hands, she wails as she scrunches the letter up and hurls it into the open fire.

"Evie — your voice?" says Grandpa, stunned as he looks from Evie to the letter burning in the fire.

Evie takes off and races outside to find Rhino. She runs blindly, searching for him, trying to find her Rhino. Tears stream down her face as she stumbles through the long, wet grass.

Rhino hears her footfalls before he sees her. He raises his head and knows immediately that something is wrong. He huffs as he trots to her. He snuffles her face and licks away her tears. Hurrying to the fence, Evie scrambles up onto his back and away they gallop down the paddock.

Rhino eases up when they reach the creek. He stands on the banks with Evie astride him, hugging him. He bleats to her, distressed by the sound of her crying.

Grandpa soon appears on Bernard, both horse and rider huffing and puffing. Dismounting, Grandpa moves towards her, but Evie puts her hand up to halt him. Evie rises to a standing position on Rhino's back and raises her small clenched fists above her in the air. She's red-faced and furious. Her cheeks are tear-streaked and blotchy and her hair hovers around her face like a halo.

Rhino remains very still, but turns his head and stares at Grandpa.

Evie feels something unbearably hot rise up into her throat. She knows then and there, it's happening. She takes a deep breath and lets go of something inside of her, something aching and black she's been holding onto. Everything she's suffered. Her body goes limp, but then it roars back to life with anger and she lets it go with a heart-wrenching cry.

Grandpa's shoulders begin to shudder and shake. He sobs silently, his expression worn and weary.

Rhino closes his eyes and throws his head back, joining Evie in a bellow full of love and loss and sorrow.

Evie puts her hand on her heart and, taking another lungful of breath, she screams again. She screams for her mama and for her papa. She screams for all the things they should be doing together. She screams for Rhino, her fears for him and her fierce love for him. She screams for the baby elephant, separated from its mama, lost and alone, and for the little monkeys taken so far from their home.

Evie screams with all her strength, until all the pain, all the aching blackness that filled her is gone, until there's nothing left inside her.

With tears trickling down his cheeks, Grandpa walks towards them. He stands before Evie and opens his arms.

"Oh, Evie. Come to me, my darling girl," he sobs.

"You can't have him," Evie cries, in a desperately thin voice. "I won't let you have him. You can't take him and give him to that awful place."

"At last," Grandpa sobs through his tears. "Your voice..."

It's a bittersweet moment and Evie can't help herself as she continues to plead and cry. She goes on and on until finally her voice breaks, dropping to a raspy whisper.

"He's mine and I love him. And he loves me. He's happy here and so am I. Please don't take him from me, Grandpa. *Please* don't let them take him away from me. *Please*, Grandpa."

Grandpa steps forward. "I love him, too," he says, and he reaches for Evie.

She slides off Rhino's rump into Grandpa's open arms. Both fear there's no way out of this. That there's nothing they can do. That the zoo owns Rhino.

"We'll get through this, Evie. We've done it before and we'll do it again. Just you and me. Rhino will be fine, he's a kindly fellow and he'll adapt to life in the zoo," says Grandpa. "We can go and visit him." But as they cling to each other, Grandpa's words ring hollow in Evie's ears.

Rhino makes a strange, strangled bleating sound. He nudges at them, pushing between them as he snuffles and licks their faces.

Evie and Grandpa laugh through their tears and scratch his neck and tickle his ears. They know Mr George Henley from the Royal Melbourne Zoo will be arriving soon to take Rhino away for ever.

It's the first time Rhino has heard the golden-haired child bellow. And bellow she did, loudly, with frustration and then anger. Impressive, for such a small human. She bellowed and bellowed until she was completely empty, until the blackness inside of her was gone. She's free, but it's left her as empty as a husk. The human child wants something with all her heart. He can sense a yearning. There's a fragile weakness to her tone as she begs and pleads. He doesn't know what it means. If he knew, he'd help her. He'd do anything for the golden-haired child. He can't stand it and bleats to calm her, to reassure her. He snuffles her face and tries to lick her pain away.

CHAPTER 21

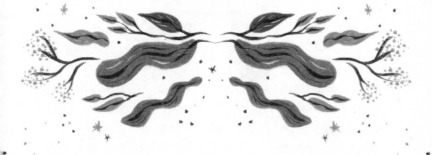

The next morning, a bellbird calls as Evie dresses. Normally, she loves to listen to their magical chiming, but she's awoken heavy-hearted with a raw throat. She dwells on the loss of the baby elephant and sighs. And then Evie remembers the zoo people are coming and there's nothing she can do about it. She swallows. Her throat feels tender since regaining her voice, but she feels different, lighter. Her voice lacks any real power, but Grandpa reassures her it will return in full.

Claudette and Florette burrow deeper into the quilt, but Albine flaps her wings and hovers from the chair to the floor, hopping after Evie as she dresses and heads downstairs.

CRESTED BELLBIRD
OREOICA GUTTURALIS

Lives in acacia scrub, eucalyptus woodlands, marram grass and sand dunes. Male 20 cm. Orange-red eyed, with a distinctive call, high-pitched and heard from some distance. Sometimes pairs duet.

At breakfast, Cook makes her a honey and lemon tea to soothe her sore throat.

"Oh, Evie. I'm so happy yer voice is back, child. I 'ave ter admit, I was bleedin' over tryin' to guess what yer wanted, although I've always fancied meself as a bit of a mind-reader."

"Thank you, Cook," says Evie, wrapping her arms around Cook's waist.

"Yer welcome, child," says Cook, enveloping her in one of her hugs and kissing the top of her head. "Git orn with yer now."

Evie begins her chores in the stables, touching Rhino's nose in greeting. She leaves the stall open, so he and Dominique can wander out at their own pace. She lets Bernard out, patting him gently on the forehead as he plods out.

The little monkeys swing down from the loft. They're obviously feeling much better, as they tug at her clothes and dance around her. Albine stays well clear of their grabbing hands.

Evie can't resist wrestling in the hay with them. They play until she's laughing and puffing and panting. She lets them run their little fingers through her hair and fossick through her pockets. They peer into her mouth and examine her ears, which they never seem to tire of doing.

Simon and Mini's understanding of Evie's cues improves every day. They watch her with their hazel eyes. They remain quiet when she asks them to "shush". Most of the time, they keep still when Evie asks them to "stay". They definitely know the meaning of the word "yes" but the word "no" is a work in progress. The stealing of apple pies has thankfully ceased as Cook is baking mini pies just for them every morning.

As there's no one about, the little monkeys accompany Evie on her chores. They love collecting the chicken eggs. Searching for them in the hay is a grand game, but Evie has to intervene when Simon starts flinging the chickens off their nests and into the air. There's much squarking and squawking about such undignified treatment.

"No, Simon," Evie says to him, shaking her head. "You do it like this, quietly and carefully, without upsetting them."

135

He watches Evie slip her hand under a sitting chicken to remove an egg. He gets it immediately and copies her.

"Yes. Well done, Simon," she says and he gives Evie another one of his gummy grins.

Evie smiles as the monkeys grab at her hands, wanting to hold them. She swings them off the ground as they walk to the dairy. Hanging upside down from the rafters, they watch Evie milk Dominique, and when she lets Francie and Freddie out, they insist on giving the dogs the "once over".

At first, Francie and Freddie are uncertain. Simon and Mini can come on a bit strong, but the dogs sit very still as little monkey fingers sift through their fur, picking and nibbling at good-gracious-knows-what. They poke inside the dogs' ears and probe inside their doggy mouths. Humiliatingly, they insist on checking beneath their tails.

At last, Evie finishes her chores. She gives the little monkeys their breakfast back in the hayloft.

A strange fluttery feeling hovers inside of her. Evie feels uncertain and she knows why. It's Rhino. He's become so precious to her, and the little monkeys have brought her incredible happiness. But she's weighed down by the waiting. Waiting for the zoo. They're due any day now, and it's the not knowing that's the hard part to live with. And, of course, what's going to happen to them when Mr George Henley arrives?

CHAPTER 22

Two days later, on the morning of 7 September, Mr George Henley of the Royal Melbourne Zoo arrives in Breamlea.

Grandpa and Evie heard of Mr Henley's arrival earlier in the day, courtesy of their neighbour, Mr Milne. He was in the village when the coach limped in. He told them Mr Henley looked weary from his journey as they had to go the long way to avoid flooding and were bogged on several occasions. He claimed Mr Henley couldn't understand the simple directions to Lunar House. He also told them the zoo handlers and the bullock dray hadn't arrived, that apparently it was so heavy and cumbersome it kept getting itself bogged to the axles. It would still be several days away.

Evie let go of a breath sitting high in her chest. This means Rhino won't be taken from her today.

Later that afternoon, Evie and Grandpa stand closely together under the ancient front portico of Lunar House, waiting for Mr Henley to arrive. Low clouds are swirling and the moisture hangs heavy in the air. There's another storm coming.

Grandpa tugs at his tweed jacket and tie and blinks in a nervous kind of way. Evie slips her hand into his, and he squeezes her fingers, peering down at her with a smile.

They soon hear the *clip clop* of horses' hooves and the turn of wheels. A filthy mud-splattered coach trundles in through the front gates, jerking to an abrupt halt in front of them. Even though the coach is battered and covered in muck, Evie can tell it's a fine one, pulled by two even finer horses.

The coachman doffs his cap at Grandpa, before securing the reins and pulling on the wheel brake. He climbs down from the coach to open the door to reveal Mr George Henley. A red-cheeked, dishevelled-looking young man tumbles out onto the driveway.

George Henley is reedy thin, and tall and gangly, in a baby giraffe kind of way. He has dark purple circles under his eyes and his clothes are dirty and rumpled. His hair looks like a bird's nest.

He's nothing but a lad, thinks Evie. *A boy.*

Hardly the grown man she imagined the zoo representative to be. There's a haunted, troubled look about him.

Evie ducks behind Grandpa, peering around him to stare at the young man, who is now picking himself up from the driveway.

Standing up, George runs his hands over his jacket, smoothing it down and composing himself before bowing to them.

Grandpa steps forward. "Good afternoon. You must be Mr Henley," he says, holding out his hand.

"I am," says George Henley, shaking Grandpa's hand stiffly. "But it's n–n–not a good afternoon, Mr Strahan. I have been d–d–driving around the countryside for hours looking for Lunar House," he stammers.

Evie is surprised by his stutter, but even more so by his anger. She glances at Grandpa; he's aware of it too.

"Some lunatic from the post office sent us on a w–w–wild goose chase. We attempted to cross the creek at three different places before we found somewhere else to cross in entirely the opposite direction. It's been a–a–a most unfortunate journey."

"I do apologise, Mr Henley. The weather this time of year makes it difficult to navigate. My family and I are isolated by floodwaters here every winter, but we're quite used to it. Please may I introduce to you, my granddaughter, Evie."

Mr Henley gives a quick bow to Evie. "How do you do, Evie?"

"Do come in out of the cold," says Grandpa, standing back from the door to allow their visitor entry. It's warm inside and Mr Henley removes his hat, gloves and coat.

Grandpa ushers him into the study where a fire is roaring in the grate. Mr Henley stands before it rubbing his hands together.

"Well, w–w–where is it?" says Mr Henley.

"I beg your pardon?" says Grandpa.

"Where is the r–r–rhinoceros?"

Evie feels Grandpa stiffen beside her. His eyes narrow as he considers the young man before him.

George Henley is as prickly as an echidna, thinks Evie.

Even though Grandpa is affronted, he answers with politeness. "Of course. Unfortunately, he's not here at the moment."

"What? W–w–where is it?" asks Mr Henley, his voice rising.

"His name is Rhino and he's out grazing. He spends most of his afternoons out in the paddocks with our milking cow, Dominique, and our old coach horse, Bernard. They're wonderful companions. They'll wander back in at dusk."

"W–w–w–what? A cow and a horse ... and he hasn't harmed them?" Mr Henley looks alarmed.

"Oh, Lord, no. Rhino's very mild-mannered."

"And he'll just w–w–wander back in?" stutters Mr Henley, laughing and waving his arms around. Evie thinks he looks a tad crazy.

"Oh, yes. He's a creature of habit."

Evie watches Mr Henley deflate. He looks at them pleadingly, with bloodshot eyes.

"My job is to bring the rhinoceros back to Melbourne. I just need to see it. That's what I have been sent here to do."

"I understand, Mr Henley, but they haven't returned as yet. And you won't be going anywhere this evening. For starters, the bullock dray isn't here and added to that, we're in for a significant weather event."

"We're in for a w–w–what?" stammers Mr Henley, looking more exhausted than ever.

"A south-easterly gale-force storm is brewing. You won't be going anywhere for at least a few days," says Grandpa, tapping the barometer on the weather gauge.

"Oh, you're serious. So, I'm s–s–stuck here?" says Mr Henley, in a wobbly, uncertain voice.

Evie glances at Grandpa and he winks at her without Mr Henley noticing.

"That you are, Mr Henley."

CHAPTER 23

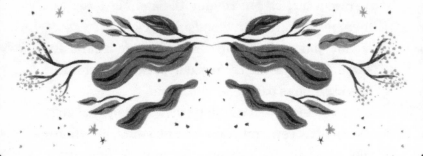

Mr Henley's knees give way beneath him, but luckily a wing chair is behind him. As he sits down – well, collapses, really – the chair makes a soft "foofing" sound and feathers float up through the air around him. Mr Henley doesn't see them as his eyes are closed.

Evie watches George Henley with interest. She has never seen anyone quite like him. He's half-boy, half-man, well-dressed yet dishevelled, confident yet accident prone, well-spoken yet a stutterer.

After a moment, Mr Henley opens his eyes.

"Mr Strahan. Evie. Please allow me to apologise to you both." Mr Henley's voice is quavery and he rubs his face. His hands are trembling. "I–I–I've been rude to you both. I'm exhausted from my journey, but my manners have been i–i–inexcusable."

"Apology accepted," says Grandpa. "I hope you don't mind me saying, you look like you haven't eaten in days. May I get you something to eat and drink?"

Mr Henley nods. "Thank you, Mr Strahan. I haven't eaten since the day before last," he says and his head flops back against the chair.

As Grandpa leaves the study, Mr Henley inhales deeply. Evie knows he's caught a whiff of the delicious aroma wafting from the kitchen. Cook left a lamb stew for dinner and before she finished up for the day, she also prepared an upstairs room for their guest.

As Evie drags a small table in front of the fire for them to dine on, Mr Henley's stomach grumbles.

"How old are you?" asks Evie.

Mr Henley opens his eyes. "I'm recently eighteen years. How old are y–y–you?"

"I'm ten years," says Evie, stroking Albine.

"I remember being ten," sighs Mr Henley, without a glimmer of happiness.

"You must have loved growing up in a zoo?" asks Evie, stroking Albine's wings.

Burk burk.

"Not really. I'm n–n–not very good with animals," says Mr Henley. "Come to think of it, I'm n–n–not very good with humans."

Evie sees something in the depths of Mr Henley's eyes. A flicker of sadness. She wonders what he's seen and, quite suddenly, feels sorry for him. Have they been too quick in judging Mr Henley?

Evie leans forward and pats his hand, like Cook does when she wants to comfort her. "My grandpa is nothing but kind."

Mr Henley glances at Evie with surprise and he gives her a small, grateful smile. The frown lines on his forehead disappear and his shoulders droop as he sinks into the wing chair.

Grandpa arrives back with a tray of food, placing it on the table between them. He pours Mr Henley a generous glass of wine.

"To warm you," says Grandpa, passing it to him before taking a seat opposite. "We've made up the blue room upstairs for you. It's the third room on the left. You'll be very comfortable, but please don't hesitate to ask for anything you need."

"Thank you, Mr Strahan. I–I–I can't tell you how exhausted and starving I am."

"Only a brave man attempts to travel at this time of year, Mr Henley. I never venture out in August and September. It's too wet and cold for me."

Mr Henley takes a mouthful of the stew and sighs.

Grandpa and Evie grin at each other as they eat. It's not the first time Cook's food has received this sort of response. The stew is hot and meaty and hearty and Evie can feel it spreading its warmth throughout her entire body.

"This is delicious," says Mr Henley.

"We live like kings here, Mr Henley, thanks to our wonderful housekeeper, who excels at cookery. We couldn't do without Cook."

"Goodness. I would love to meet her. I–I–I actually have a strong interest in cookery."

"What sort of interest would that be, Mr Henley?"

"Well, I love to cook myself, Mr Strahan. I w–w–would love to be an accomplished cook."

"A chef perhaps?" asks Grandpa.

Mr Henley blushes the colour of beetroot and he nods as he swallows another mouthful of stew. Evie sees Mr Henley hesitate, as if he wants to say something more.

"At present, I've been put to work in administration by my father. I'm actually afraid of animals, large animals anyway. I do like birds though, I–I–I mean, who doesn't? To fly must b–b–be incredible!" laughs Mr Henley, stuttering. "I'm sorry. I'm talking a bit too much. Anyway, my dream is to be a chef, much to my father's disappointment."

"Disappointment?! A chef is a marvellous profession. To have a calling in life means you will live happily. I believe in callings. I was called by the wonder of birds into ornithology. My son, Evie's papa, was called to veterinary science by his love of all creatures great and small. A calling is a good thing."

Mr Henley stares at Grandpa's open enthusiasm and honesty with wide eyes. He nods his head vigorously and raises his glass in agreement. Grandpa raises his in return.

"Well, then, Mr Henley. Tomorrow you shall meet Cook."

Their guest exhales in a rush and stammers, "Please, M–M–Mr Strahan, and you too, Evie. Please call me George."

Grandpa and Evie glance at each other. She wonders if they're both thinking the same thing – that George Henley isn't too bad after all.

CHAPTER 24

Over the next few hours, Evie watches George as all his prickles disappear. He's actually quite charming and his stuttering lessens until it's almost unnoticeable. She can't believe it's the same person who tumbled out of the coach and onto the driveway.

"Well, now, Evie. One shouldn't judge on appearance alone, eh?" says Grandpa.

He's right, thinks Evie. *George Henley is pleasant. Even if he is here to take Rhino. Oh no, Rhino.*

Evie's heart sinks. For a few moments, she'd forgotten why George was here. She excuses herself, and slips out of the house and into the stables. Rhino's in the foaling stall with Dominique sharing a bucket of bran and molasses. He sees Evie and moos, tossing his head. Evie smiles and strokes his nose. His rubbery lips nibble at her fingers and, as she scratches his chin, she contemplates George Henley.

Evie feels she should hate George, but finds she cannot. He has a round, open face and he speaks to her with frankness, giving her his full attention. He makes her feel seen and heard. Meeting George hasn't been as difficult as she expected.

Maybe he will take care of Rhino? wonders Evie.

She climbs the ladder to the hayloft to check on the monkeys. They're sleeping entwined and even though they seem to be snug and warm, Evie pulls another horse rug over them. She strokes their downy hair and sweet little faces. Their injuries are healing well and Evie's noticed they've lost that hollow look they had about them. She grins, thinking it must be Cook's apple pies.

Evie kisses Rhino good night as he snuffles and inhales her hair and face. She hurries back to the house and pauses at the study door to listen to Grandpa and George.

"Evie is a delightful child. She seems older than her ten years," says George.

"She's been through a great deal," says Grandpa. "Her parents drowned in a shipwreck two years ago. Robert was my only son, and Isobel was like a daughter to me. It was a huge blow. For both of us."

"I'm sorry for your loss," says George.

"Don't worry about Evie. She's smart and she's fearless, as you shall witness tomorrow. She has a natural affinity with animals and a unique ability to communicate with them. Evie has a gift, like her father before her. And, dare I say this to you, she is very attached to Rhino. And he to her."

Evie sighs. Hearing this comparison to her papa makes her feel like laughing and crying at the same time.

"I see," says George, uncertainty in his voice. "Well, in the morning, I'm very much looking forward to meeting this rhinoceros."

Evie slips back into the study, plonking herself down on the rug in front of the fire with Albine. The rain outside begins to hammer down in earnest and George stares into the fire. She sees a wave of sorrow pass over his face. A fire can do that to a person, make them remember sad things.

I wonder what's making George so sad? thinks Evie.

"Did you know, Evie was the one who found the rhinoceros on the beach?" Grandpa says to George.

"Good Lord, I did not," says George, turning to Evie. "Weren't you scared?"

Evie shakes her head. "Oh, no. He is the kindest of all animals."

"I see." George is quite taken aback. "How did

you manage to get it back to Lunar House?"

"He followed me." Evie stares at George with her enormous blue eyes.

"She led him by the horn," adds Grandpa, the beginnings of a small smile tugging at his lips.

George shakes his head. "Remarkable."

"Evie, tell George about your recent bird sighting."

"Oh, yes, please do," says George.

"Rhino and I saw a pair of orange-bellied parrots. They're rare, thought to be extinct."

"How marvellous. How would you describe them?" George leans forward in his chair.

Evie sits up, animated. "They're colourful and they have an unusual bird call."

"How so?"

"It's a buzzing sound. Like an insect."

Evie heads to the bookshelf. She retrieves *The Birds of Australia* as she tickles Claudette under the chin. She also grabs another book, a green cloth-covered folder. Its spine is worn and it contains every ornithological academic paper published by C.H. Strahan.

"Well done, Evie. A budding ornithologist, eh, Charlie?"

"Oh, no. Evie's quite the seasoned expert."

"Grandpa's library is one of the most comprehensive ornithological collections you'll ever see," says Evie, puffing her chest out.

THE BIRDS OF AUSTRALIA

1. SPOTTED PARDALOTE 2. TAWNY FROGMOUTH 3. GREY PLOVER
4. BLACK-THROATED FINCH 5. RED-TAILED BLACK COCKATOO

George rises for a tour of the bookshelves with Evie. She shows George the near extinct orange-bellied parrot in *The Birds of Australia*, and Grandpa's recent illustration.

"This is incredible, Charlie. There are books on your shelves I've never seen before. Tell me, you must know my father?"

One of Grandpa's eyelids twitches. If you didn't know him well, you might have missed it, but Evie didn't.

"Who's your father?" asks Evie.

"Well, as you know, he's the director of the zoo, but he also wrote this," says George, holding up *The Birds of Australia*. "About twenty years ago."

Evie stares from George to Grandpa, with wide eyes and a gaping mouth. A light flickers on inside her brain. She takes the book from George and flips *The Birds of Australia* over and stares at the spine, and there, embossed in gold, is the author, D.L. Henley.

Douglas Henley is George's father! I knew I'd seen that name somewhere before.

Evie shivers. *Why have I not made this connection before? Something isn't right here. Could this be the reason why Grandpa loves this book, but also why he can't stand it?*

Grandpa inclines his head. "I do know your father, George. I used to know your father very well. We served together in the Ornithological Society and the Acclimatisation Society of Victoria."

A look of concern washes over George's face. "I didn't know that. My father never m–m–mentioned it to me, and yet he was the one who sent me here. Don't you think that's odd...?" George says with a sense of unease.

"Well, to be fair, the correspondence regarding the shipwreck didn't have my name on it. Your father wouldn't know I live here. We haven't seen each other for a long time."

"But why are you no longer involved in either of the societies, Charlie? You obviously still have so m–m–much to offer."

"The Acclimatisation Society collapsed twenty years ago and reformed without me, as the Royal Melbourne Zoological Society. It's all right, George, if there's one guarantee in life, it's that nothing stays the same. Everything changes."

Evie can't believe her ears. She is listening to Grandpa explain all of this to George without a hint of bitterness in his voice. He's actually smiling as he speaks.

And then it dawns on Evie, whatever happened all those years ago, Grandpa no longer cares about it. But the problem is, that Evie does. There's a whiff of injustice and she's going to find out exactly what happened. She can tell by George's face, a mixture of shock and disgust, that he isn't convinced either.

"But why, Charlie? I don't understand why you were so blatantly left out."

"It's complicated, George. Oh, don't worry about me. I'm happy with my life. Would you like to go for a ramble tomorrow? With all this low-lying water we have an abundance of birdlife."

"That would be wonderful. Will you come too, Evie? I'm sure I'll need your help identifying birds."

George looks so keen, Evie feels she can't refuse and nods her head.

"It's bed time, my dear girl," says Grandpa. "Come on, I'll walk you upstairs."

A loud peal of thunder claps overhead, followed by a flash of lightning.

George flinches at the sound, but notices it has no effect on Evie.

"I love storms." She grins at him. "Good night, George."

"Good night, Evie."

Leaving the study, the cats leap down from the shelves and slink after them. As they climb the stairs, Grandpa carries Albine like a baby and Evie hugs *The Birds of Australia* and Grandpa's academic papers to her chest.

Evie loves reading about birds before she nods off and, as Grandpa tucks her in and kisses her forehead, he whispers, "Don't read too long, my dear girl."

But when Grandpa closes the door, Evie reaches into her bedside drawer for her emergency stash of candles. Claudette and Florette leap onto the bed and claw at the quilt, as if they're kneading dough, before snuggling in close.

Evie places *The Birds of Australia* and Grandpa's academic papers on either side of her. Albine *burk burks* in her sleep and Claudette and Florette softly purr, as she reads long into the night.

CHAPTER 25

The next morning, Evie awakes as confused as she was upon falling asleep. The wind howls around the chimneys of Lunar House, but she can still hear wrens tittering in the eaves outside her window.

She pats the sleeping forms of Claudette and Florette and, as always, their purring is a comfort to her. She stares at the watermark on the ceiling above. Another tile must have blown off during the night and the roof has leaked. She'll have to push her bed to the other side of the room and she makes a mental reminder to tell Grandpa about it.

Even though Evie knows *The Birds of Australia* by heart, last night she decided to read it again from the very beginning to the end. Upon finishing each chapter, she cross-referenced it with Grandpa's published academic papers. Up until chapter five, all was going along swimmingly. But when she arrived at the spotted pardalote, her world fell apart. Evie rubbed her eyes and re-read the description of the bird three times. Each time, the text was exactly the same as Grandpa's. Word for word.

It was as she suspected. Grandpa was betrayed by a friend. His friend, Douglas Henley, published Grandpa's work as his own.

This is the reason why Grandpa's always had mixed feelings about *The Birds of Australia*. It's her favourite book and she pushes it in his face all of the time. Evie cringes. *How hard this must have been for him? Poor Grandpa.*

Then it dawns on her that this would also be the reason why Grandpa didn't want to put his name on the telegrams when he was reporting the shipwreck.

Mr Douglas Henley is a despicable man. But what sort of a person does this make George? Is the son like the father? He doesn't seem to be, but can we trust him to take care of Rhino?

Evie wishes she could test George somehow, to find out what sort of person he truly is.

She eases out from under the quilt so as not to disturb Claudette and Florette. Albine nestles on a chair in the corner and as Evie kneels to stroke her comb, she coos and sways in her sleep.

Evie needs time to think about everything she has discovered about this secret. She isn't sure about anyone or anything any more, but she is sure about one thing – she doesn't trust Mr Douglas Henley.

CHAPTER 26

As Evie sits on the bottom of the stairs, pulling her boots on, she hears voices in the kitchen.

Cook and George are chatting away in there like old friends. For the last couple of years, there's only been Grandpa, Evie and Cook and Mr Duffer. She's never had to share them and she feels a grim, jealous feeling unravelling inside of her.

George is seated at the kitchen table as Cook fusses around him with plates and napkins. He rambles on and on. "When I went up to my room last night, I found a hot stone in my bed. For the first time in w–w–weeks, my frozen toes were warm," George laughs. "Thank you, Mrs Tait."

"Oh, 'tis me pleasure. Please, call me Cook, everyone else does."

"Well, then. You must call me George."

"Oh, no. I couldn't do that," says Cook, as she dishes George up his breakfast.

"I don't think I've enjoyed such an evening, not with my father, or the cranky old cronies at the zoo."

"'Tis true. Mr Strahan is great company. He's intelligent. And the child, Evie, is as smart as a whip. Do yer not git on with yer father, lad, if yer don't mind me askin?"

Evie pricks her ears up at this.

"My father has little time for me, he never has. I don't think he holds much regard for me," says George, as a matter of fact.

Cook tut tuts. "I'm sure that's not true, lad?"

"Oh, it is, Cook. It is. And the feeling is mutual. I've given up trying to please him. Oh, my, what is this?" says George, taking a bite into his breakfast and changing the subject.

Evie leans her head against the banister. She cannot believe what George has just said. And he said it with such resignation, like he's known and accepted it for a long time.

Poor George. He's not like his father at all. But can I trust him?

Evie puts her head in her hands. How can I protect Rhino? How can I stop this from happening?

"It's a *croque monsieur*," says Cook.

"Please, Cook, what is this amazing cheese?" George asks with sincerity.

Cook retrieves her old family cookbook, drags out a chair and launches into what Evie knows will be a long-winded conversation about her cheese-making process, about how cheeses are made on farms all over England. Every family recipe has been handed down for generations. Differences in flavour and texture are due to the landscape of the region and the breed of cow that families keep in their herds. Cook's family proudly made a traditional cheese called "Taiter Crumbly", a very tasty cheddar. George leans forward in his seat and listens intently to Cook.

Evie races upstairs to her bedroom and retrieves *The Birds of Australia* and Grandpa's academic papers. She thinks if George is as indifferent to his father as he says he is, then reading the pages she's marked shouldn't cause him any further grief than his father already has. *Or will it?* she wonders. She shakes her head, jumps down the stairs, two at a time, landing with a thud in the kitchen. She plonks the books down onto the kitchen table and slides them in front of George.

"Good morning, Evie," says George, his face flushed and happy.

"When you're done here, you should read these," says Evie, tilting her head and eyeing him with meaning.

"Oh, all right, Evie. I–I–I will," stammers George, looking bewildered. "Thank you."

Evie dashes from the house and leaps onto Rhino's back. They race down the paddock towards the creek, with Dominique and Bernard trailing close behind.

As they gallop, Evie thinks about what she's done. She is relieved at sharing her secret and realises this is the test she's been hoping for. And if George does the right thing and passes it, there might yet be hope for Rhino.

CHAPTER 27

A few hours later, Evie and Rhino turn for home. They gallop up the gentle rise from the creek, against a backdrop of green fields and a grey thunderous sky. Her hair flies in the wind, bouncing on her back in time with Rhino's stride. When she sees two dots in the distance, she waves. She knows it's Grandpa and George.

Clicking her tongue, Evie uses her hands to guide Rhino, and they head towards them.

Evie sees George stiffen as they ease from a gallop to a canter, a canter to a trot, from a trot to a plodding walk.

"Whoa," says Evie, sliding from his back, and landing with perfect balance on her feet. Grandpa has an amused look in his eyes, while George is pale. His lips move without any sound coming out, and he blinks several times.

Rhino is puffing and snorting and his flanks are heaving from the exertion.

"H–h–he ... is ... enormous," stammers George.

"Isn't he magnificent?" says Evie, with one hand resting on his shoulder. "Come say hello."

George stares at Rhino and Rhino stares at George, narrowing his eyes.

"I–I–I'll stay back here ... if that's all right?"

Evie smiles at him. "Of course, but Rhino won't hurt you. He's friendly."

"But ... but don't they charge at you? And gore you with their horn? I'll just look at him from here."

"Let's walk back to the house," suggests Grandpa, smiling to himself. Their boots squelch as they sink into the sodden ground.

Evie and Grandpa and George wander into the garden and sit in the love seat of the rose arbour. A sliver of wintery sun peaks through the clouds and they turn their faces to it, soaking it up as Rhino and Dominique graze.

Claudette and Florette arrive from the study, blinking and squinting in the sunlight. Albine appears, scritching and scratching around Rhino's feet. Francie and Freddie bound in, tails wagging. They flop down on the grass beside them, half watching them, half sleeping in the sun.

"I've never seen a rhinoceros before," admits George, breaking the silence.

"Impressive, isn't he?" says Evie. "He's the kindest of animals."

George gives a half nod in agreement. He's uncertain about Rhino, and Evie stares at George trying to work him out.

"Rhino is big-hearted, but some bulls can be feisty," says Grandpa.

"Oh, yes, of course," George gulps, his Adam's apple bobbing up and down. "How is it, Evie, that you're so good with animals?"

"I love them," says Evie. "I'm always with them."

"W–w–why aren't you at school?' asks George, studying her.

Evie looks up shyly. "Well, after Mama and Papa died, I lost my voice. Words just wouldn't come out and everyone at school teased me. Rhino is my best friend. We like all the same things, exploring the beach, tumbling down sand dunes, wandering the paddocks, playing down at the creek. And he loves cows and old horses and cats and dogs, and he really loves chickens."

Burk burk says Albine.

Evie glances at Grandpa sheepishly and he pats her hand. They both know she should return to school soon.

"I can relate to that, Evie. I was teased at school after my mother died."

"Is that when your stutter started?" asks Evie softly.

"It was," says George, giving her a small, sad smile.

Birds chatter in a tree nearby. They hover before swooping the snoozing Francie and Freddie. The dogs sit up, annoyed at being awakened, barking at the birds as they dive-bomb them.

"They're wattlebirds," says Evie. "They're cheeky and always teasing the dogs."

George watches Evie pick up Albine and stroke her chest.

"You would have thought growing up in a zoo, I'd have been happy. But I wasn't. My mother died when I was ten years old. I was so lonely and wished for my own dog. But I wasn't allowed a pet."

"Why not?" says Evie, believing this to be terribly unfair.

"I can still recall my father's words. '*You live in a zoo, you idiot. You don't need a pet – you're surrounded by them.*' But European wolves aren't exactly the same as a dog. They snarled and bared their teeth at me, licking their lips whenever I would wander past."

Shivering, Evie blurts out, "Your father is evil."

"Evie! Where are your manners?" says Grandpa, a look of surprise on his face.

"No, Charlie. My father is not a good man. It's well known, as you, I suspect, have known for a long time. I appreciate you trying to protect me from it. But I'm a grown man now and believe me, I've lived with his meanness most of my life."

Evie places a small hand on George's arm. They lock eyes and what she sees reflected there is a mirror of her own sorrow and heartache. A moment passes between Evie and George. She understands him and he understands her.

Evie feels a small fluttering inside. She remembers this feeling, the strange warm, uplifting feeling of hope.

George holds Evie's hand and gives her a wobbly smile. At this very moment, he couldn't look further from a grown man.

"George, I'm so sorry," says Grandpa. "Douglas wasn't always like that."

"It all began when my mother died, and when I met Gerta. My dear, sweet Gerta."

Evie and Grandpa glance at each other, wide-eyed.

Gerta?

CHAPTER 28

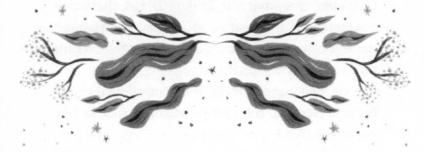

"Who was Gerta?" says Evie, sitting cross-legged on the grass with Albine *burk burking* in her lap. The cats have taken up on either side of George, leaning against him, purring, as they groom and lick their paws.

"Gerta arrived at the zoo when I was ten."

My age, thinks Evie.

"Gerta was an African elephant, a matriarch of her species. She was magnificent, graceful and kind," says George, smiling at Evie.

I love elephants, too. Evie sighs. She thinks she's now finally accepted the fact the baby elephant didn't make it ashore after the shipwreck, but it still haunts her dreams.

"Gerta was the new star attraction at the zoo. As a temporary measure, she was housed in the old seal enclosure – they'd all died because algae kept growing in the water. It had been drained and converted into an 'enclosure' of sorts, but it was a concrete bunker. Windowless and dank, a dreadful place to keep any animal," explains George, with a pained expression on his face.

Evie feels uncomfortable about this story. It's causing her stomach to float around inside of her. Grandpa's face is grimacing and she knows he feels the same. He looks at her with a sadness in his eyes. He holds his arms open to her and she clambers up onto his lap.

"Not long after Gerta arrived, a handler brought out a long, sharp stick with a hook on the end that's used to control elephants. Well, Gerta took one look at it and pulled against her chains. She'd seen one before. I saw the whites of her eyes; I knew she was scared." George whispers this last word, as if he didn't want them to hear it.

"I visited Gerta every day. I'd take an apple or handful of grass and, one day, I plucked up the courage to touch her. I remember feeling astonished at how warm she was. She kept her eyes closed; I'm sure she was imagining she was elsewhere, anywhere but there."

Evie looks at Rhino. *Does he wish he was elsewhere?* She can't answer this, but she does know

Rhino doesn't stand around with his eyes closed. He's wide-eyed and always wandering off wherever he fancies, in the garden, in the paddocks with Dominique and Bernard and he visits his wallow daily. He sleeps in a warm stable beside Dominique and is watched over by the ladies. He's not caged or fenced in, he's free to roam, and he's surrounded by people who love and care for him. Of course, it's *not* his real home, but it is a home of sorts. Evie hopes he's found some sort of happy.

Rhino stops munching on grass. He glances up to find all three humans staring at him. The golden-haired child, the old human and the young nervous one who has recently arrived. A sadness hovers over him like a storm cloud. But it is the small human child who is staring at him with the greatest intensity. This is not unusual; she often clutches at his head and gazes deeply into his eyes as she questions the world. He shakes his head, curling his pink lips to show her all is well. He knows he is safe, there's plentiful food and the company is excellent. The humans turn their attention back to the young nervous one. He begins to tell a story, and Rhino can tell already it is not a happy one. Sounds struggle to be free from him and his heart is trembling.

Rhino huffs. The nervous one quakes and quavers, shrinking into himself like a pangolin. He is not one to face things. There is tragedy in this story and Rhino watches as the human child turns her face away to burrow into the old human. Rhino burps softly, lowers his head and watches on respectfully through his eyelashes. He cannot turn away, just in case the golden-haired child needs him.

Evie looks back to George. She doesn't want to listen to him, but finds she can't stop herself. He takes a shaky breath and continues.

"I begged my father to build Gerta an enclosure with trees and grass and, for once, he paid attention to me. But it wasn't long after one was built that a zoo handler poked Gerta once too often with the hook. He went flying and was dead before he hit the ground. Gerta was back in the bunker, this time with her feet chained to the floor."

Evie feels tears spill from her eyes. Tears for Gerta. Tears for George. She buries herself into Grandpa's jacket, and inhales everything that is safe; bran and molasses, smoke and ink.

George exhales a shaky breath and talks on, ever so quietly, ever so sadly. "You see, Gerta was captured as an adult. She'd known freedom in her life and they never forget it. She was tortured by the memory of it and by the time I met her, she hadn't been happy for a long time. Gerta took up a constant, hypnotic swaying, rocking from side to side for hours on end. She never opened her eyes again, nor did she eat again."

"She willed herself to die," whispers Grandpa.

"And so I refuse to work with zoo animals. Because of Gerta's suffering. Because I couldn't save her."

"George, you were a little boy. You were ten years old. This wasn't your fault, my boy."

George stares up into the sky. "I've got to head into Breamlea first thing in the morning to find out where the zoo handlers and bullock dray have got to."

Grandpa nods.

Evie stares up into the same sky. She knows now there's no way she can allow Rhino to go to the zoo. He wouldn't survive.

Clouds are swirling and gathering above Lunar House. Evie's mind is swirling and gathering. And then, like a bolt out of the blue, a solution.

If Rhino disappears, then they can't take him away.

CHAPTER 29

The following week a southerly wind, straight off Antarctica, blasts Lunar House. It's not so much wet, as it is icy cold. Squally winds and skiffy rain rarely abate, yet the days disappear in a blur of all things Rhino.

George found out the bullock dray is holed up in Geelong for repairs. He mentioned something about a cracked rotating shaft and some missing bearings. Evie feels blessed for the delay and the extra time she has to plan where she's going to conceal Rhino.

Cook and George spend their days in the kitchen busily working their way through every recipe in Cook's cookbook, and Grandpa works in the study.

When they can, Evie and Rhino escape to the beach, exploring the marshes and playing down at the wallow. They even spend a day following the meandering creek until it meets the Thompson River, tracing its path until they sight the village of Breamlea.

All this time, they're scouting out places, hidden, isolated places, where one could hide a very large rhinoceros. But Evie hasn't found one yet that she believes is entirely suitable.

When it's been too miserable to go outside, they bunker down in the stables together, continuing to plot and plan.

But Evie's aware time is running out for her and Rhino. She has no idea when George is leaving and yet she cannot settle on a spot to hide Rhino, and plays out different scenarios in her head, trying to cover all bases for things that could go wrong. So much so, she's now angry with herself. She's wasting time, she has to take action, she has to protect Rhino.

What am I waiting for? wonders Evie. Yes, it's wintery, but that shouldn't stop her. It's never stopped her before.

Sniffling and lost in her frustrations, Evie looks up to find Rhino staring at her. She wipes her eyes on her sleeve and gazes back at him. His eyes are full of trust and he blinks at her, acknowledging her fear.

The golden-haired child is full of worries. They dance around inside her like fireflies. Rhino can see the strain around her eyes. But it's not sadness, or grief, it's something else. Her heart is fluttering erratically. He stares right into her eyes and focuses on the deep well of courage he knows is inside her. She has already shown much courage for her tender years. The challenges they face are many. But they are stronger than they think. Rhino continues to stare at her, sending her his strength, willing her to believe in herself. He believes in her. He trusts her.

Evie touches Rhino's nose and closes her eyes. She tilts her head slowly forward and as their foreheads touch, she solemnly commits every bone, every muscle and every fibre in her being to the protection of Rhino.

Evie sends Rhino a message. *I'm going to do this, I won't let you down.*

Rhino licks her hand, and burps loudly.

CHAPTER 30

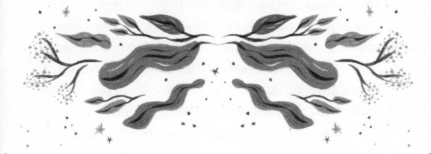

The weather conditions at Lunar House continue into the following week until the wind direction changes into a south-easterly gale. A storm is bearing down upon them, and Grandpa taps the weather gauge in the study with his finger. With a roaring fire, a delicious dinner of shepherd's pie, and apple pie for dessert, the three of them are cosy.

Grandpa is writing a paper, his first in twenty years, about the orange-bellied parrot. Evie starts drawing the greater one-horned rhinoceros, but ends up moving on to rhesus monkeys, and George is thoroughly engrossed in reading Cook's old family recipe books.

Claudette and Florette lie sprawling in front of the fire and Albine is perched on her favourite cushion in the wing chair, her eyes hooded. Every now and then, she *burk burks* in her sleep, swaying and jolting herself awake.

Evie feels the temperature dropping as another freezing cold night seeps in around them. She's worrying about the animals in the stable. Simon and Mini, in particular, feel the cold.

"Grandpa, the barometer has dropped very low," says Evie. "Might we light the forge in the stables?"

Grandpa taps the barometer again. "Of course, Evie. There's going be a frost. I'll go and do it now," says Grandpa rising from his chair.

"I'll come and help you, Charlie," says George, and the two men leave the room.

For some reason, Evie stops drawing, and her pencil hovers in mid-air. She puts it down, and tip-toes after Grandpa and George into the inky black, cold night.

The stables are chilly and her breath puffs in white clouds. She tiptoes into the feed room and wraps herself in a horse rug, crouching in the doorway to listen.

The forge, a brick-lined fire pit, is set in the middle of the stables. Next to it lies an anvil and an assortment of hammers and nails and rods of iron to smith into horseshoes.

Grandpa uses a flint to light the kindling and the

fire takes with a whoosh. It crackles and pops and casts a shadowy, orange glow inside the stables.

"Here, George. Crank this handle for me, will you?" says Grandpa.

George pumps the bellows to feed the flames.

"Keep doing it until the timber chars and forms coals. It'll keep the stables warm all through the night then," adds Grandpa before going to check on the animals.

Bernard sleeps while standing and sways as Grandpa passes. In the foaling stall, Rhino and Dominique nestle side-by-side in the straw, softly snoring.

The ladies *burk burk* when they see Grandpa, and Rhino lifts one sleepy eyelid in acknowledgement.

Grandpa touches him on the nose before returning to George, who is leaning against the warmth of the forge. Grandpa rubs his chin and blinks several times.

"I have to ask, George," says Grandpa, "you've been at Lunar House now for, what, two and a half weeks? And, well, I'm wondering when you're planning to take Rhino?"

Evie squeezes her eyes shut. This is what she's been waiting for, this is what she's been dreading.

George stutters, "I–I was waiting for the floodwaters to recede. That bullock dray bogs at the drop of a hat."

"I think the roads are mostly safe to travel on again," says Grandpa.

George nods and swallows.

"The longer Rhino is here, the more attached Evie becomes to him. I don't want to hurry you or ask you to go, George, but I've got to know your plans."

Evie breathes out, pressing her knuckles into her mouth.

George inhales and exhales. "I'm sorry, Charlie. I know I've been putting it off. I–I ... I like it here. I like it here so much, I haven't wished to leave."

"And we like having you, George. Let me assure you, my boy, you will always be welcome here. Always." Grandpa grasps George's shoulder. They stare into the fire and Grandpa speaks with measure, wanting to make his meaning clear to George. "You must understand, I need to prepare Evie for her separation from Rhino."

Tears tumble from Evie's eyes and she bites down on her fist to stop herself from crying out.

"I know, Charlie." George's voice is despairing. "I understand. This situation doesn't sit well with me either. I've thought a great deal about what Evie has been through with the loss of her parents. And what you've been through, Charlie. I–I–I'm terrified I'll let Rhino down. And you and Evie."

"You won't, George. You're an adult now and there's no way you would let what happened to

Gerta happen again. Zoos are different places these days, too. And Rhino is a placid fellow. He's grown up in captivity, so he won't be any trouble. And you'll be there to make sure he's fine."

"But what if something happens? You don't know what my father is like."

"None of us know how strong we are until being strong is the only choice. The darkest times bring out the best in people. You're a good lad, George. Goodness always prevails."

"I'll go into Breamlea tomorrow. I'll find out where the zoo handlers and the bullock dray are. It's time to get myself organised." George nods.

"Yes, it is, George. Thank you."

As Evie wipes her tears away, her heart sinks deep inside of her. She cannot trust George like Grandpa can. *Yes, he's a good person, but his father isn't. If George can't protect Rhino, then what will become of him?*

Evie is furious with herself. She's dillydallied for far too long. She must put her plan into action immediately, she has to stop this from happening!

CHAPTER 31

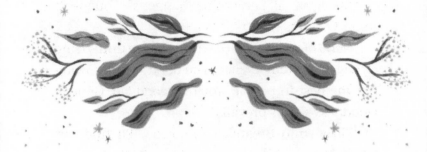

The following morning when Evie awakes, her mind is whirring with her plan. She's ready to go. Outside her bedroom window, it's overcast but she can see the sun trying to push through the clouds. Before she can put her plan into action, Evie must do her chores so everything appears normal.

As she opens the door to the stables, mayhem greets her. Simon and Mini are going wild, swinging from the rafters and hooting and screeching.

"Come down here," calls Evie.

They bare their teeth at her, and jump and leap around her, just out of arms' reach. They swing into the hayloft and begin tossing bundles of hay down to the ground.

Evie stares at Rhino and he stares back at her as if to say, *What do you want me to do?*

"Stop! Stop it, Simon! Mini, come down here now!" calls Evie.

The little monkeys trapeze between the rafters and continue to swing back and forth and back and forth. Evie watches them, twirling and whirling, swinging to and fro, thinking, *They're very impressive!*

Evie gasps and puts her hand over her mouth as Simon lets go of the rafters. He somersaults and spins through the air, tumbling and falling, before landing upon Rhino's back. He grabs hold of his ears and pulls them hard. Rhino receives such a

shock, he roars and takes off, tearing around the stables at breakneck speed.

Mini also drops from the rafters, landing as light as an acrobat on top of Dominique, who moos in fright and takes off around the stables. Evie's grateful Bernard is out in the yard.

She doesn't know what to do so she opens the stable door. Rhino charges through it with Simon on board, clinging onto his ears. Mini rides astride Dominique. Her bell is clanging and banging as they tear around the yard.

"No! Stop!" wails Evie, feeling helpless. Simon and Mini are out of control. She has to stop them, but they're not listening. They're dodging and darting, always remaining just out of arm's reach for her to catch them.

Passing the clothesline, the little monkeys leap from Rhino and Dominique's backs onto the clothesline. They swing along it, and begin pulling off the washing!

Pop, pop, pop. Pegs fly into the air.

One by one, Simon and Mini fling the clothes off the line, tossing them into the garden.

"Stop! Stop it!" hisses Evie, waving her arms, trying not to attract attention from inside the house. She doesn't think Grandpa will be able to hear the commotion from the study, but Cook in the kitchen might.

Sure enough, Cook appears at the kitchen door.

"What's all the racket?" says Cook, taking in the scene. "Bloomin' heck!" She spins on her heels and hurries back into the house, only to bump into George. She stands in such a way that she blocks the view from the door.

"It's just Evie, clangin' a bell to scare the cockies off the veggie patch, like I asked her to," Cook explains to George. "Rhino's helpin' her and so is the daft cow."

Rhino reappears by Evie's side, puffing and panting with his nostrils flaring. From deep inside his belly comes a growling sound.

"I didn't know cockatoos were such a problem?" Evie hears George ask.

"Absolute pests, they are," says Cook. "Come into the pantry, lad, I want to show yer some spices..." says Cook, her voice trailing off as they fade back into the house.

Rhino puts his head down and snorts, before pawing at the ground with one foot.

"Oh, no!" says Evie.

Rhino takes off, and charges at the monkeys.

"No, Rhino!"

Rhino skids to a halt, no less than a centimetre from the clothesline and the little monkeys' faces. Simon and Mini gape at him, with surprised, wide hazel eyes. He inhales before bellowing directly into their faces. He moos with such gusto, Evie sees their hair blow up off their heads, like a stiff breeze, only grassy smelling.

Whether it was the volume or the force of Rhino's bellow that stopped the monkeys in their tracks, Evie doesn't care. Simon and Mini drop from the clothesline and sit beneath it looking meek and bewildered, obviously in some sort of shock.

Evie watches as the little monkeys' attention quickly turns to Bernard, who is standing harnessed into the buggy.

"Oh, no, you don't. Don't even *think* about it," snaps Evie. They hurry towards her, hanging their heads. "So you should be," she says, gathering a monkey in each arm, returning them to the stables and shutting the door.

CHAPTER 32

After pegging the washing back up on the clothesline and tidying up the hayloft, Evie feels like her day has disappeared. But it's not lunchtime yet; there's still plenty of time to put her plan into action.

Mr Duffer appears at the stables and Evie helps him to harness Bernard to the buggy so he can take George into Breamlea to find out where the zoo handlers and the bullock dray have gotten to.

"Don't worry, Evie. I'm going to put them off for as long as I can," George tells her. But with his father being the way he is, Evie can't help but doubt George's good intentions. She feels the bullock dray could be here any day now.

"Come on," says Evie. Rhino saunters along behind her, through the wild garden, under the rustling moonah trees, over the bumpy hummocks and into the sand dunes.

Evie collects a pile of driftwood and it's in the seclusion of the sand dunes she chooses to build an enclosure for Rhino. On one side is basalt rock, which creates a natural barrier. The other side of the dune needs a fence to complete the place that will hide Rhino. With a rock, Evie bashes mainstay posts deep into the sand and it is through these she weaves driftwood to form a fence.

While she works, she lectures Rhino in a firm voice.

"You must stay here, out of sight. Do you understand me?"

Rhino watches Evie, huffing over her shoulder.

But Evie finds the driftwood difficult to bend. It's brittle and easy to snap, and her fingers are full of tiny splinters. She sucks on them and continues working.

By mid-afternoon, the semblance of an enclosure is taking shape. Feeling happy, Evie returns to the stables. She finds George, recently returned from Breamlea, in the garden, picking herbs with Cook, and Mr Duffer in the house paddock repairing a trough. It wasn't easy but Evie did several trips to the stables, without anyone seeing her, returning to the dunes with armfuls of lucerne, a bucket of bran and molasses and a bucketful of water.

This might work, thinks Evie, and she leads Rhino inside the enclosure, shutting the makeshift gate. She props a few rocks against it, to make sure it's solid. Rhino stares at Evie doe-eyed.

"You must stay here until I get back. Do you hear me?"

He curls his lips at her, making a smacking noise.

"I love you, too. Now, stay." Evie gives him a quick kiss before scampering back towards the house.

Rhino sniffs at the strange stick fence and leans against the gate. It's as flimsy as straw, but for some reason the golden-haired child wishes him to stay here. He will, for her. She never does anything without a reason, so he'll go along with it. For now. Until he runs out of food. Or if the urge to wander overcomes him, he may have to leave. It happens when the breeze brings him delightful smells that call to him. Call him to investigate. Sometimes, the call is irresistible. But, for now, he'll stay in the sand dunes as asked.

When Evie returns to the stables, she finds Mr Duffer cleaning out the foaling stall and replacing it with fresh hay.

Simon and Mini hear her and poke their little heads out of the hay. She waves her hands at them to "stay put" and shakes her head at them.

"Rhino's missing. Have you seen him, Mr Duffer?"

Behind Mr Duffer, Evie can see the monkeys hanging upside down from the loft.

Mr Duffer leans on his pitchfork and scratches his head. The monkeys swing high into the rafters of the stable roof, and Evie forces herself to look Mr Duffer in the eye. *At least they're not chattering,* thinks Evie.

"No, Evie. I haven't seen him since he headed off with you into the sand dunes earlier," he says.

Evie nods and hurries to the house where she finds Cook and George sitting together at the kitchen table. They're reading recipes and George is copying them out by hand into his notebook.

"Rhino's gone. I can't find him anywhere," she announces to them.

"I'm sure he's down the way, child, grazin' with that daft cow," says Cook.

George looks up. "Have you seen Dominique, Evie? They're always together."

Evie rushes to the study to seek out Grandpa.

"Rhino has gone missing. I can't find him anywhere; I've been looking for him all morning. He's gone, Grandpa. I'm sure of it."

Grandpa looks up from his desk where he's working. "Are you sure, Evie?"

"Quite sure. He's gone. He never wanders far. What if he's lost?"

Grandpa turns to the window and smiles. "Well, I'm sure I can see him wandering in from the sand dunes."

"What?!" Evie dashes to the window where she sees Rhino sauntering into the garden, nibbling parsley, and twirling his tail.

CHAPTER 33

Rhino is so huge and magnificent, Evie knows it's going to be difficult to contain him.

She stares at the ploughing harnesses hanging on the stable wall. She touches them. They haven't been in use for a long time but they are still strong. She remembers the plough being pulled by two enormous Clydesdales. She heaves on the harnesses, letting them fall to the ground. They're heavy and land with an almighty clank.

Albine and the ladies scatter and Simon and Mini start to hoot, the loud noise alarming them. They swing down from the loft and clamber onto Rhino's back, pointing at the chains on the ground.

"It's all right, Simon and Mini," says Evie, reassuring them as she checks the stable door to make sure no one else heard the noise. It's been three days since the morning of wild mayhem and all has been forgiven between Evie and the little monkeys. They seem more settled with life at Lunar House. When Evie goes into the stables in the mornings, they're always snuggled in their blanket in the loft. They then happily follow her around and help out where they can. When she tells them to "shush" and "stay put", they do. She's not sure how long it will last, as they are, after all, cheeky monkeys.

"Come on, Rhino. We've got to make this work."

Rhino stands, chewing on his pink gums, as Evie attempts to harness him into the contraption, minus the plough. He doesn't mind having chains draped all over him. He even has a little snooze while waiting for Evie to finish whatever it is she's up to, and lets Simon and Mini poke around in his hairy ears.

Evie peers around the stable door again to make sure nobody is around. She shuts the monkeys in and leads Rhino down the paddock towards the creek. The chains clunk and clank in time with Rhino's gait and Evie breathes a sigh of relief. *This might actually work.*

The creek is a long way from the house and not in view through any of the windows. Evie loops the chains around a tree beside the creek and sits and watches Rhino rub his horn on it and nibble at the bark. She rubs her hands together, which are now not only full of splinters, but blistered from handling the chains.

She steals back to the stables for food and water. The tree will provide Rhino with adequate shelter and if he eats all the lucerne, he can graze on grass until she returns tomorrow with more food.

Evie's halfway down the hill when she sees a flash in the corner of her eye. She spins around to see Simon and Mini dart past her.

"You two are so naughty," says Evie. She lets them go. She doesn't mind the little monkeys coming with her. They do love an outing.

When they arrive at Rhino's tree, Simon and Mini climb high into the branches, peering down at her with serious eyes. She smiles up at them, letting them know she's not cross.

Evie and the little monkeys remain with Rhino for the afternoon, chatting and playing.

"Now, you must stay hidden, Rhino. Otherwise, George will take you to the zoo in Melbourne. And you don't want to go there, trust me. I'm doing this for you. When George leaves, I'll set you free again and that could be very soon."

At twilight, Evie grabs Rhino by his furry ears and kisses him good night.

"I promise I'll see you in the morning. Come on,

little ones," Evie calls Simon and Mini. They swing down to the ground and she holds her arms open to them, but they hesitate. They keep running from Rhino then back to Evie, until Rhino shakes his head at them, snorting.

Simon and Mini hang their heads and clamber into Evie's arms. She cuddles them and carries them, one on each hip, back up the hill to the stables.

As Rhino rubs his rump against the rough bark of the tree, he ponders the reasons why the golden-haired child is behaving so strangely. Her eyes are darting, her pulse is racing and there's a desperate edge to her voice. He wishes he could persuade her otherwise. So he lets her drape him in heavy irons and walk him down the paddock to the creek. The stink of mud is delightful and delectable, and he considers leaping in. But she coils the irons around the tree like a python. If she thinks this will contain him, she is sadly mistaken. The human child knows little of his strength but he realises he's never exerted it before in front of her. It might be time to do so. He huffles, thinking about the warm fug of the stables. He has become accustomed to comfort. But for now, he will stay here as she bids.

He is uncommonly loyal. But the monkeys are unhappy. He tosses his head at them, reassuring them he shall return in due course, probably when he becomes hungry.

Cook stops Evie in the doorway of the kitchen and gives her the eye. She tut tuts as she reaches forward and touches her stockings, checking to see if they're dry. "Where on earth 'ave you been, child? Yer been gone all bleedin' afternoon."

Evie whips her hands behind her back so Cook can't see them. "I've been looking for Rhino. He's gone missing again."

George appears with a concerned expression on his face. "Oh, no, he hasn't has he?"

"He'll be somewhere around 'ere," Cook says to both Evie and George. "Do not fuss yerselves. Now, I need to take Mr Duffer a cup of tea," she says. "I'll ask 'im to take a look fer the daft thing. Go an' wash up, Evie. It's almost dinnertime."

George pats Evie on the shoulder. "He won't be far away, Evie."

"As if a rhinoceros *can* git lost?" mutters Cook as she heads off to find Mr Duffer. "Can't the monstrous, great thing look after itself?"

Evie's hands are tender and she winces as she

washes them for dinner. She pushes them deep into her pockets before visiting Grandpa in the study. He's in his wing chair reading by the fire. Albine perches on the opposite chair, and Claudette and Florette are in the bookshelves.

"Albine and I have been wondering what you've been up to all afternoon, Evie." Albine *burk burks* as if to confirm this fact and Evie's face breaks into a small, sad smile. Grandpa holds his arms out to her.

Evie climbs up onto his lap and rests her head on his chest. She can smell bran and molasses and smoke and ink. All things safe. She closes her eyes and counts his steady heartbeat. She wants to tell him the truth, about where she's hidden Rhino and about the monkeys. She wants to, but she can't. She has to carry this out, she must stay the course if she's to protect Rhino.

"Rhino has disappeared. I've looked for him everywhere."

"Goodness, again? I'm sure he'll turn up. He's like a homing pigeon, isn't he? He won't be too far away."

Evie can't bear to look at Grandpa in case he can see the truth in her eyes. He knows her so well and she keeps her eyes downcast.

"What's worrying you, my dear girl?"

"Nothing, Grandpa."

Grandpa touches her sore hands. "You know,

whatever it is, I can help make it right. You only have to ask."

Evie snuggles into him and her splintery thumb drifts into her mouth.

No one can help me. Evie stares into the blazing fire and prays with all her might Rhino will be all right.

CHAPTER 34

Evie's sleep is fitful and plagued by awful dreams of Rhino calling out to her. Claudette and Florette snuggle in, but for once their purring doesn't soothe her.

Moving between sleeping and waking, she must have dropped off at some point in the early morning.

Evie wakes late, her eyes red and scratchy. Then she remembers. Rhino! Chained to a tree down at the creek. *What was I thinking?* She was trying to protect him, but by chaining him up it occurs to her that she's acted no better than George's own father. And Evie despises George's father! She sobs as she dresses, accidentally tipping the sleeping

Claudette and Florette from the bed. They meow and complain as she fumbles and hops around before toppling poor Albine off her chair as well. Dressed at last, Evie rushes outside to bring Rhino home.

But the household is already up. In the kitchen, Cook and George are weighing ingredients for whatever culinary delight they're making for dinner tonight. They don't even look up as she streaks past them.

"It's all right, Evie," says Grandpa, waylaying her at the kitchen door. "Mr Duffer and I have done your chores. There's no need to worry. But you were right about one thing. Rhino is missing. He didn't return to the stables last night and there's no sign of him this morning."

Evie's heart sinks. She hops from foot to foot, anxious to take off running down to the creek.

"We should do a reconnoitre of the farm," says Grandpa.

By now, Evie's almost teary in her desperation to run.

"Let's split up, it'll be quicker," he adds.

"I'll go down to the creek," says Evie.

"I'll walk the beach. Let's meet back here in an hour."

Evie sprints through the house paddock, nearly colliding with Mr Duffer who is coming through the gate in the other direction.

"Whoa. Evie, good mornin' to yer," he says, dodging her.

"Good morning, Mr Duffer."

"No need ter rush, lass. I've seen Rhino. He's wanderin' up the hill. Reckon he's been in a bit o' mischief overnight – he'd got himself all tangled up in chains, the silly bugger. They've dropped off now though, somewhere down the paddock."

"Oh," says Evie, puffing and so relieved she's unable to form any words.

Grandpa reappears then, panting. "Mr Duffer, Evie and I are searching for Rhino and—" he stops to take a breath.

"As I was saying to young Evie here, Mr Strahan, Rhino will be along in a jiffy. He's comin' up the hill, taking his sweet time with that darn cow. Never in a hurry, those two."

"Oh, good news," says Grandpa. "How is Rhino?"

"Fit as a fiddle," says Mr Duffer. "I'll tell you what though –" he steps through the gate – "I've seen a strange thing. A blackwood tree has come down by the creek. It was healthy last time I saw it. It'd be nigh on ten years old and it's been clean sawn off at the base."

"How peculiar."

"'Tis, but who's to say it wasn't rotten at the base, Mr Strahan? We've seen that happen after floodin'."

But Evie knows full well it is not the reason.

The tree was fine the last time she saw it too. *Rhino must have pulled so hard on the chains trying to free himself that he sawed the tree in half.* Evie whistles low and slow. She's surprised at Rhino's strength; she should never have chained him to a tree.

Her heart soars when she hears Rhino before she sees him. He and Dominique are mooing and bellowing as they wander up the hill. As they near, Rhino grins and calls out when he sees her. He looks perfectly well and cheerful.

"It's good to see he's his happy self, Evie," says Grandpa before he heads back to the house.

He's hungry, Evie thinks to herself, knowing well Rhino's *I'm starving, please feed me* moo.

In the stables, Evie dotes on Rhino while she feeds him breakfast, and begs him to forgive her. He snuffles her hair and licks her face as if there's nothing in the world she could do that would ever need forgiving.

Simon and Mini swing down from the hayloft and they too fuss around Rhino.

Rhino slugs down an enormous amount of water from the trough. He gobbles down three buckets of warm bran and molasses and munches through six bales of lucerne.

Evie decides to make one last attempt at concealing him.

Leading Rhino by the horn, and with Simon and Mini riding on Rhino, Evie walks him to their neighbour's property. The grass is knee-high and swishes around their legs. They walk upon a flock of ibis feeding upon grubs and the birds flap their wings and squawk, before taking off.

Simon and Mini flap their arms, imitating the birds.

Milne's dairy is as Evie remembers. It's a large stone building, quite hidden from view, and warm and dry inside. It is here Evie plans to leave Rhino until George goes. There's plenty of water and hay and straw and, even better, cows for company.

"You'll be safe here. Please stay, Rhino. Stay." Evie wags her index finger at him. "I'll be back to visit you later." Rhino stares at Evie and lets out a sigh as if to say, *Not again*. But he stays where he is, sniffing his new quarters and nibbling on hay.

Simon and Mini are reluctant to leave Rhino, but with much coaxing they follow Evie back through the paddocks.

When she appears in the study that afternoon, Evie finds she cannot sit still. She can't concentrate on reading or drawing. She feels herself trembling inside.

"Evie, what is wrong with you, child?" says Grandpa.

She's not sure if it's the warmth of the study or the awful feeling she's done something wrong, but Evie feels quite unwell.

"I'm sorry, Grandpa. I've left something in the stables."

She dashes outside.

On the kitchen step, Evie's breathing is fast and shallow. She tries to slow it, tries to keep herself together. And then, who should appear in the yard before her, wearing the silliest of grins? Rhino, with two cheeky little monkeys sitting on top of him.

Evie walks Rhino to the stables, and into the foaling stall with Dominique, and carries Simon and Mini to bed up in the hayloft. As she closes the stable doors, Grandpa appears in the yard.

"Evie, my dear girl, are you feeling all right?" he says opening his arms to her.

She nods, relieved Rhino's home – and one of Grandpa's hugs is just what she needs.

CHAPTER 35

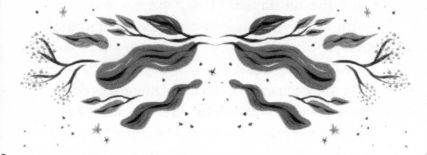

It's early morning, the day after Evie's third failed attempt at hiding Rhino. George told her yesterday he'd managed to continue to delay the zoo handlers in Breamlea for another week by requesting additional repairs to the dray.

Evie knows she should be grateful, but as she opens her eyes to the warbling of magpies, she pulls the covers up over her head. As Claudette and Florette purr in their sleep, she realises she's not capable of hiding Rhino. He's too enormous, too strong and too friendly. She knows now she can't protect Rhino. And George can't keep the zoo handlers and the bullock dray at bay for ever. Her stomach wobbles and she sniffles into her pillow.

Evie is slow to rise, she feels sluggish and listless. She dresses and goes downstairs, with Albine ruffling her feathers and hopping down the stairs one at a time *burk burking* after her.

On the kitchen step, Evie is conscious of how much she loves Lunar House in the early morning. Frosty and misty and silent. Soon the sun will come up making everything silvery and sparkling.

In the stables, she touches Rhino's nose in greeting and he sniffs and snuffles her, licking her hand. She lets him and Bernard out to graze, and Simon and Mini help her collect the eggs. She milks Dominique and lets Francie and Freddie out, who bounce around her. As Evie kneels and scratches the dogs' silky ears, she gazes past Freddie only to see Paddy Tait wander into sight. He's standing in the yard, his postal satchel slung across his shoulder.

Evie sucks her breath in. *This can only be bad news.*

"Top of the mornin' to yer, Evie," says Paddy, waving to her. Evie gives him a limp nod and watches as Paddy bounds up the steps, into the kitchen.

Evie plods after him, placing the milk and the eggs in the pantry.

Cook is cooking George breakfast, but she can tell something is wrong. There's more than a chill in the air as Evie dashes to the study to find Grandpa.

"I'm coming, Evie. Slow down," says Grandpa, puffing as he follows her back into the kitchen.

Evie retreats into the hallway to listen. She plonks herself down on the bottom stair, and drops her face in her hands.

"Sit down, George, yer look pale," says Cook, her voice full of concern. "Will yer stay, Paddy, for a cuppa?"

"No, thanks, cousin. I'd best be orf," says Paddy. Sensing the tension in the room, he reverses himself quietly out the kitchen door.

"What's happened, lad?" asks Grandpa.

"I've got a message from the zoo handlers in Breamlea," says George, holding it in his hands.

"Go on, then, my boy. Open it. Whatever it is, we'll handle it," says Grandpa.

As Evie hears the tearing of the envelope and the unfolding of paper, she wraps her arms around herself.

"It can't be that bad," says Cook, trying to reassure George, even though she's heard all about his dreadful bully of a father.

George gives a long, shaky sigh and opens the note. Cook twists her hands in her apron, her eyes darting from George to Grandpa.

"The zoo handlers are bringing the bullock dray here. The day after tomorrow. There's to be no arguments. No more delays. My father has ordered it," says George, sounding defeated.

"What?" says Cook, with alarm.

George starts gasping for air.

"All right, lad, slow down now. One breath in, one breath out," says Grandpa, rubbing George on the back.

"I've got to pull myself together. I–I've enjoyed myself so much here with you, Charlie. And Evie and Cook and Mr Duffer and Rhino. I've been selfish. You're all so kind to me. I haven't wanted to bring the bullock dray out to Lunar House because when I do, this all comes to an end."

"It doesn't have to end, George," says Grandpa. "You're always welcome back here, my boy. Always."

George is sobbing now. "But what about Evie? What about Rhino? I'm going to let them down."

Evie hears the broken resignation in his voice.

"Come 'ere, lad," says Cook and embraces George in one of her smothering, air-depriving hugs.

Evie rushes out to the stables to Rhino. He's napping in the foaling stall and she snuggles in against him, clutching his head. He snuffles her hair and licks her face. Simon and Mini hover around, stroking her hair. They're eating little monkey-sized apple pies and their fingers are sticky, but Evie doesn't mind.

A single tear rolls down her cheek. Like George, Evie too finds herself feeling resigned. The fight is out of her. The fight is over. So she waits. Waits for this to all come to an end.

Rhino is dozing as the golden-haired child bursts in through the stable door like a whirlwind. At first, he thinks the child has been galloping but she's hiccupping and wailing as she gasps for air. He licks her face to calm her and her tears taste like honey. He can taste her anguish. The monkeys are also aware the small human child is in a state. It's upsetting them as well and Rhino nudges at them with his head. He huffles around them all, nuzzling them in close to his side, bringing them in to the crook of his neck so they can lean against him. He has broad shoulders, he just wishes he knew what he could do to relieve the child's fears and the growing darkness inside of her.

CHAPTER 36

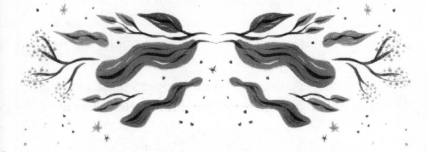

An hour later, Evie wanders into the kitchen to find the entire household in disarray. Everybody is walking around on eggshells, not knowing what to say to each other.

George is in his room upstairs and they can hear him pacing back and forth. Grandpa has shut himself in the study because he's worried about what's going to happen to Evie when Rhino is taken away and Cook is in the kitchen cooking up unnecessary quantities of food because everybody is in distress, including her!

Nobody can look at Evie, let alone say anything. Finding the right words is never easy, as she knows. She spins on her heels and runs upstairs. She has to tell George she's going to be all right, that she understands that he has a job to do. He has to take Rhino away. She taps on his door, but there's no answer. She knocks louder.

George cracks open the door and at first doesn't see Evie. His eyes are bleary and bloodshot, and his hair is all over the place. He looks terrible, like he hasn't slept in days.

"Evie, I..." George's mouth opens and closes like a fish gasping for its last breath. He hangs his head.

No words, thinks Evie. *He doesn't know what to say to me.* Evie can't bear the awkwardness between them.

"When are you—?" she goes to ask George.

"I have to t–t–take—" says George, stumbling over his words.

"When are you taking him?" Evie rushes her words in one breath.

"I'm sorry, Evie. I've tried to delay the zoo handlers, but my father is demanding we leave. I love it here, but we have to go."

"I know. But can I ask you a favour?"

"Anything, Evie."

"Can you make Rhino a big enclosure, one with lots of grass and trees, like the zoos in London and Paris? Can you make it as large as you can?"

George swallows and nods and they stare at each other for a few moments, before he looks away.

211

Evie sees the flicker of doubt. She dwells on this – George is fearful of his father.

"I know you'll look after him. I trust you, George. I didn't before, but I do now."

"Why are you saying this, Evie?"

"Grandpa says you will look after him."

George nods. "I'm not a brave person, Evie. But I will do my very best for Rhino."

Evie attempts a wobbly smile and pushes a big toe against the rose-patterned carpet.

"I know what you were trying to tell me when you asked me to read your grandpa's academic papers," says George.

"Oh," says Evie. For a moment the world tilts and a wave of sorrow hits her. She feels sorry for Grandpa and for Rhino. And sorry for George, since these problems all rest on his shoulders.

"It all makes sense to me now," says George, pacing his room. "I know my father stole Charlie's work. I know that's why he excluded Charlie from the Zoological Society. That's why he's had so little to do with the Ornithological Society since. I have to find a way to make this right, Evie. I want to make things right for Charlie, for you and for Rhino. I–I–I–just don't know how. I want to take a stand against my father, but I'm not sure..." says George, his eyes filling with tears.

George is so confused, thinks Evie. *He can't seem to make sense of his situation and doesn't know how to make his way forward.* She's at a loss as to how to help him.

"Evie," George whispers. "You're the bravest person I know. How can I find the courage?"

Evie reaches her hand up and places it on George's chest, above his heart. She can feel it beating. It's strong. Stronger than he thinks.

"It's here, George," says Evie. "Your courage, is right here. It's always been here."

CHAPTER 37

Evie takes the stairs two at a time, relieved George knows the truth about what his father did with Grandpa's work. He's taken it better than she thought, but he's seen this behaviour before so he's not shocked by his father's dishonesty. *George has definitely passed the test*, thinks Evie, but what he does with this information now is up to him.

Evie's given herself a headache thinking about all of this and she hurries outside to find Rhino. She tracks him down with Dominique and Bernard. They're grazing together under the cypress trees in the house paddock. The three of them are standing side-by-side, so close they could be touching, like pieces of a puzzle.

Rhino stops chewing and lifts his head when he hears Evie coming. His ears swivel and flick and Evie touches Rhino's nose in greeting. He snuffles her hair before yawning and huffing his grassy breath all over her. The two of them stare at each other.

They don't need any words and she wraps her arms around his neck and leans into him, breathing in his earthy scent. She snuggles into his warmth and strength and whispers into his ear.

"I will never forget you. Ever."

Rhino waddles over to the fence for Evie to clamber up onto his back and they gallop to the beach.

Rhino grunts as he goes up the dune but they rest at the top, taking in the view of the bay. He watches as Evie raises her arms above her head and turns her face to the sea. Inhaling a lungful of air, she screams. Rhino follows her lead, huffing in a deep breath before bellowing with similar gusto.

She grins at him before tumbling down the face of the sand dune with a one-tonne, very nimble Rhino close behind her.

Two pied oystercatchers skip in front of them, taking off over the water. They wail their sad cry, and Evie drops to her knees at the water's edge.

She scans the horizon. The swell is glassy and sluggish, unpredictable, as if it can't decide what to do next. She kneels on the shore with her eyes closed. Beside her, Rhino is listening too. He sits quietly, his body light against hers. She places one hand on her heart and reaches out with the other to touch Rhino's neck.

I know you're there, Mama, Papa.

After a long moment, Rhino blows in her ear to let her know that he, too, is there. She opens her eyes and hugs him.

Rhino can feel the golden-haired child is savouring a moment, like he savours the divine stink of his wallow on a stiff breeze or the delightful scent of new shoots of grass or the cloying reek of fresh chicken manure. He knows what it is to savour. But there's a bitter tang to the human child. There's sorrow inside her, mingled with grief and loss. He huffles her hair and licks her face. She always smells delicious, of milk and honey. Of all things good. And everything the human child is feeling, he understands. But she needs to understand this – once we are loved, we are never forgotten.

Rhino farts explosively and Evie rocks back on her heels and laughs.

Instead of grieving for Rhino, which Evie will do well enough when he's gone, she promises to enjoy every last minute she has left with him. Evie wants to remember everything about Rhino. His big round head, his hairy ears, his long-lashed brown eyes and his warm grassy breath against her cheek. She will remember his bouncy trot, his wobbly bottom and his lip-curling grins. His patience, his kindness, his deep love of chickens and his loyal devotion to Bernard and especially to Dominique.

But what Evie will miss most of all is Rhino's presence. When she's near him, she feels whole again. The aching blackness that engulfed her after her parents died lifted because of him. Her voice returned, all because of her love for Rhino. And his love for her.

A lump forms in Evie's throat but she forces it away and stands up, brushing the sand from her dress. Rhino looks at her, his head to one side. She rubs his ears before running off along the beach and calling for him to follow her.

Not far out to sea, grey clouds are scudding and rolling in on top of one another.

Another storm is coming.

CHAPTER 38

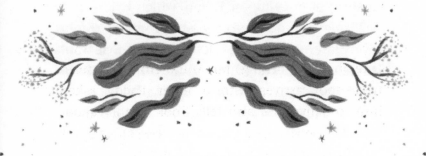

Evie and Cook are in the kitchen the next morning when George staggers down the stairs.

"George, are yer all right? Yer look awful," says Cook, fussing around him as she makes his breakfast.

"I didn't sleep well."

"I can't function if I don't git enough sleep. Here yer are, lad. Food will make yer feel better."

"Thank you, Cook. Thank you for everything." George sounds overly dramatic, and Evie notices his hands are quivering.

"I don't know what to do. My mind is a mess, I can't think straight!" George knocks his chair over backwards and leaves the kitchen in a flurry.

He returns to his room, and Cook and Evie look at each other as they hear him pacing in his room, back and forth and back and forth.

Late in the morning, Mr Milne from the farm next door arrives with a letter Paddy asked him to deliver. He also tells Cook a story about strange happenings in his dairy. The letter is for Mr George Henley, bearing the gold crest of the Royal Zoological Society.

Cook hands it to Evie. "Go orn, child. Take it up to 'im."

Evie races upstairs. She knocks on George's door and is about to slide it under, when the door opens.

"Come in, Evie," says George, his voice sounding weary. He notices the letter in her hand. "Is it from my father?"

Evie nods and passes it to him.

"I'm not surprised. I–I–I knew it was coming, I know h–h–he's angry." George moves to the window and rips it open. He grips the windowsill as he reads the letter.

Before Evie's very eyes, George begins to wilt, as if he's shrinking into himself. He passes the letter to Evie and as she skims it the world turns a little darker.

24th September 1891
c/- Breamlea Post Office
South West Victoria

George,

Where on earth are you, you stupid boy?

My men in Breamlea have told me they haven't seen high nor low of you for weeks. Where are you, George? What are you doing? My sources tell me the floodwaters have receded. Do I have to send out a search party for you and that damned rhinoceros? And where is the rotten thing? I knew I shouldn't have sent you, a boy on a man's mission. You've always been soft, you take after your mother. You're overly sensitive and make a mess out of everything. You're nothing but a lily-livered weakling! Don't you realise the zoo needs its star attraction? We're going broke, George, in case you'd forgotten? Things have gone from bad to worse here while you're lost in the wilderness.

We've cleaned out the concrete bunker all ready for the rhinoceros so send me a telegram ASAP to let me know what is going on. I need you to return to Melbourne immediately - with the rhinoceros!

Yours sincerely,
Sir Douglas Henley
Director of the Royal Melbourne Zoo,
Royal Park, Parkville

Evie's heart trembles.

The concrete bunker is ready? What is he talking about? He doesn't mean where Gerta was kept?

"I can't think. I've got to get out of here." George takes the letter back from Evie. "I'm going for a walk." With a grim expression on his face, he stumbles down the stairs and sets off for the creek.

Evie hurries to tell Grandpa and Cook about the dreadful contents of the letter. Unknown to Evie, Simon and Mini have snuck into the house and at that very moment they follow Evie to the study.

"You run ahead, Evie, and we'll catch up," says Grandpa, rising from his desk. Cook's standing at the doorway, wringing her hands when the monkeys appear alongside her.

"Good Lord ... monkeys! Rhesus monkeys?" Grandpa gapes at Evie before he begins laughing. Simon and Mini huddle in the folds of Cook's skirt.

"Oh, Evie. Where on earth did you find them?" says Grandpa, his eyes full of tears from laughing.

"Come here, my little mites," says Cook, and they leap into her arms. "Go orn, child, go bring George back ter us." Her voice quivers. "I'll sort things out 'ere."

And Evie runs. She runs to the house paddock where she finds Rhino and Dominique and Bernard. She mounts Rhino at the fence and the three of them canter down the paddock. A rhinoceros, a milking cow and an old coach horse. The animals had seen George marching past moments before, so they know where to go.

As George storms off down the hill, grass whips at his legs. At the bottom, he sits down – well, collapses really – and holds his head in his hands, taking deep breaths.

When Evie has George in sight, she asks Rhino to stop. He does and so do Dominique and Bernard. They huff and they watch and they wait.

A screeching cry cuts through the air. A wedge-tailed eagle hovers in a slipstream above. Evie's breath catches – its wingspan is at least seven feet. It's enormous and magnificent.

George is watching it too, and when the eagle flies away he rises and walks up the path in Evie's direction. He looks crazy-eyed and his cheeks are streaming with tears.

Evie waits for him on the side of the path. But when George lifts his head and looks at her, his eyes are unseeing and he walks straight past.

Quite suddenly, Rhino appears before George and steps into his path, blocking his way. Behind Rhino, on either side, are Dominique and Bernard. They too step forward.

George tries to sidestep Rhino, only to have him step across the other way, cutting him off. He makes to go the opposite way, but again Rhino prevents him from going past. They stand face to face, less than a metre apart.

George has never been this close to Rhino before and a look of terror washes over his face.

Evie's heart hammers as she watches a stand-off unfold.

George's breathing is coming in short gasps and his legs are trembling. A soft wail escapes him and his father's letter is quivering in his hands.

Rhino pads forward and prises the letter from him; his hot breath and warm lips nibble at his fingers. Rhino proceeds to eat the letter. He makes a show of it, tossing his head around, and the parchment crackles and crumples and turns to mush. With a shake of his head, he swallows it, and burps.

George is rigid with fear and they stare at each other. Rhino's eyes are long-lashed and brown and warm and, for the longest moment, George and Rhino gaze into each other's eyes.

Evie holds her breath.

"Do it." George's voice cracks and he drops to his knees before Rhino. "Trample me to death. Gore me with your horn, will you? I deserve it." He laughs a sad laugh before he begins to hiccup and tears trickle down his cheeks.

Rhino curls his lip into a grin and he shuffles forward to snuffle George's face and hair.

Placing her hand on her heart, Evie thinks of her mama and papa. She thinks of Grandpa. And Cook and Mr Duffer. And George. And his endearing ways. She thinks of the dear little monkeys. And she thinks of Rhino.

Evie experiences the strangest sensation watching George and Rhino. Something happens to George, something changes within. He gives in to Rhino. He relaxes his shoulders, his head flops forward and a deep, shuddering sigh escapes him.

Rhino plants a sloppy kiss on George's forehead. Then, with a lumbering grace, he farts and wanders off down the paddock with Dominique and Bernard.

George opens his eyes. They're clear and focusing on Evie.

"That's the most remarkable moment I've ever had in my life. A wonderful moment, with a wonderful rhinoceros!"

George laughs and Evie laughs too. It's a nervous laugh at first, like the relief one might feel after a brush with danger. Next thing, the two of them are truly laughing – belly laughing. Evie holds her sides and George buckles forward with his hands on his knees, hooting with laughter.

"If I ever had a sister, Evie ... I'd wish her to be like you. Brave and kind."

Evie blushes the colour of a ripe plum. She can't help but notice a renewed energy about George, an urgency about him that wasn't there before. He's glowing with everything that hurts and everything that he loves.

"Evie, I'm no longer scared," he whispers. "I'm no longer scared of Rhino. I'm no longer scared of my father," George yells down the hill. "I'm no longer scared!"

Evie grins at George and a fluttering of hope floats inside of her.

"I know exactly what I'm going to do now. For the first time in my life, I can see the way ahead of me. Quick, I have to get back to the house. There's so much to do," says George animated and enthusiastic.

Evie hurries after George. He's walking so fast she can hardly keep up. He's walking tall and with purpose up the hill.

At the crest, they bump into Grandpa and Cook and Mr Duffer who are waiting for them.

Grandpa's face is solemn and serious. Cook is red in the face and twisting her apron into a knot. Mr Duffer is gripping his tartan cap. They look from one another, to Evie, then to George.

"You all right, George?" asks Grandpa.

"Charlie, Cook, Mr Duffer," nods George. "I must take my leave at first light tomorrow. Charlie, I cannot thank you enough for having me. But it's time for me to leave."

Grandpa and Cook and Mr Duffer look at George and nod.

"Cook, will you help me to pack?"

"Of course, lad."

"And, Mr Duffer, will you be so kind to take me into Breamlea this afternoon? I need to get to the post office."

Mr Duffer doffs his cap and nods.

"Are you sure about this, lad?" asks Grandpa.

"I am." The expression on George's face is one of calm. They take in this expression, before hurrying off to help with his departure.

George kneels before Evie, holding her shoulders.

"I have to write a telegram and a long, overdue letter to my father. All will be well, Evie," says George. "Just give me an hour, Cook." And he races up to the house, bounding up the stairs to his room.

Who is this person? thinks Evie. George's transformation may have shown him the light, but Evie's in the dark, feeling more confusion than ever about what on earth George is going to write in his letters.

CHAPTER 39

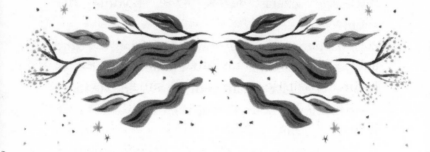

"George says he shan't be joining yer for dinner tonight, Mr Strahan. He's outta sorts," says Cook, choking on her words and waving her hand at them.

Grandpa and Evie eat their shepherd's pie in silence.

"I'm so used to seeing George sit in that chair, Grandpa. It's as if he's always been with us," says Evie, stroking Albine's tail feathers under the table.

"I agree. George is tremendous company. I shall miss him," says Grandpa.

"I'll miss George too, Grandpa, but not as much as I'll miss Rhino."

"I know, my dear girl. I know."

"Will he be all right?"

Grandpa puts his knife and fork down. "They'll both be fine, Evie. It's complicated for George. He's going through a great deal of inner turmoil. I feel for him, I really do, but he'll work his way through it. Whatever happened to him down the paddock has got him into gear," says Grandpa, raising an eyebrow at Evie. "George is not his father. He needs to believe in this himself. He can resolve this situation."

"He had a close encounter with Rhino," says Evie.

"I thought as much. He saw the light, eh?" says Grandpa.

He certainly saw something, thinks Evie.

Grandpa reaches out and touches Evie's cheek.

"Evie, you need to keep Rhino in the stables tomorrow morning until the bullock dray arrives. Don't worry about Simon and Mini, Cook will keep them out of sight. And, dear girl, you need to say your goodbyes to Rhino."

Evie nods and swallows something aching and black inside of her.

As she goes upstairs to bed, it's not possible for Evie to believe it. To believe this day is here. She stands in the middle of her bedroom, telling herself to get ready for bed. Albine fusses around her, sensing something isn't right. She finds herself taking a blanket and making her way downstairs and out to the stables.

Rhino hears her footfalls and opens an eye. Evie touches his nose in greeting and he snuffles her face and her hair, inhaling her scent. He has a dreamy look in his eye and she snuggles close to him, one arm around his head, stroking his nose.

She pulls the blanket over her and curls in against his shoulder. She can hear his heart beating. Thud. Thud. Thud. Steady and sure and strong. She inhales and exhales until her heart beats the same as his.

Rhino awakes in grey semi-darkness. Clouds are shrouding the moon and the wind plays music through the gaps in the walls. It's late and something has happened. The golden-haired child appears before him. She's as quiet as the night itself, and she's shaking and shivering. She burrows into his side like a newborn calf. What is it? What is wrong? He huffles her hair, but he can't tell what it is.

He's aware not all is right in the universe tonight. He senses something deep inside of her, aching and black. He knows this feeling too. He thought he'd forgotten about it, but he hasn't at all. He still remembers it. It's the burden of loss and he will carry it with him always.

But the smell of spices and tea of his homeland

have been replaced by that of a honey-milk-scented golden child.

Rhino sighs. He wants to protect her as if she were his calf. If he could stop whatever it is that is causing the darkness to grow inside her, he would. He huffs. If he knew, he would charge at it, trample it or gore it with his horn. He could eat it? Or maybe he could sit on it? That would fix it. But he doesn't know what it is. So, he wraps himself around her and lowers his head, cradling her little body against his.

He feels her letting go. Her breathing softens and, little by little, she relaxes and finally drifts off to sleep. He feels the tiny blip of her heartbeat slowing and his own heart lightens as they beat the same tune.

Evie's sleep may be deep and dreamless but Rhino's is unsound and broken, with images of Evie calling him weaving in and out of his nightmare.

At the darkest hour of the darkest night, when all the world is quiet and everyone is asleep, something arouses Evie. Through sleepy eyelids she's sure she sees Grandpa. He's standing in front of her in his pyjamas and slippers and his shoulders are quaking as he sobs into his hands. Evie feels Rhino stir against her and it's only then she knows she isn't dreaming.

Grandpa touches Rhino's nose, before shuffling back to bed.

CHAPTER 40

All night the south-easterly howls around Lunar House. It brings down an old gumtree and blows several more tiles off the roof. In the early hours of the morning the wind finally blows itself out.

Evie and Rhino are up early and walking on the beach. It's their last walk together. There's not a breath of wind and it feels strange to Evie not to have it whistling through her ears.

Evie carries with her a heavy heart weighed down with worry about Rhino's future. How he'll cope in captivity, being shut in a small enclosure and how he'll handle being away from everyone who loves him. But Rhino's in a chipper mood as if he's trying to cheer her up. He moos at Evie as he chases the waves. He turns and runs after her, dodging and weaving around her, snorting and huffing. He hooks seaweed onto his horn and swings it around and around in the air. It lands on his head, and it looks like he has a huge mop of hair.

Evie chases after him. He spins his tail, farts and takes off, spraying sand everywhere. His bottom wobbles as he dashes up the beach, jaunty and swashbuckling.

Returning to the stables, Evie feels like she's going through the motions, but isn't fully present. Rhino plods after her, following her into the stables as she makes him up one last bucket of warm bran and molasses. She sits in the foaling stall, watching him eat.

Closing her eyes, she listens to his rhythmic chewing and swallowing. There's a rumbling sound coming from deep inside his belly. It's a satisfied sound, not unlike a cat's purr. It's lulling, until, that is, Rhino gets to the bottom of the bucket and he tips it up onto his head and bangs it around to make sure he's got it all. Evie leans her head against his. Rhino snuffles her face.

Dominique shuffles in and Rhino swirls his tail. After a huge burp, they pad around in a circle in the straw, before settling down together for a morning nap. With one last, lingering look, Evie closes the stall door.

As soon as she walks into the kitchen, Evie feels the change in atmosphere. It's the same feeling she gets when the weather gauge drops and the barometric pressure rises. Grandpa calls it "the calm before the storm".

Evie's stomach swirls with anxiety and she can hear her beating heart.

George has been up early too, preparing to leave. He refused to take breakfast, his last at Lunar House, but he comes down to speak to Cook. Evie is in the pantry gathering breakfast for the little monkeys when George appears in the kitchen.

"Thank you for everything, Cook. Thank you for feeding me, for teaching me how to cook, for sharing your recipes. For being you – wonderful you."

"Come 'ere, lad." Cook embraces George. "I've packed provisions for yer journey." Her voice breaks as she hands him a basket full of his favourite food.

George walks through the hallways of Lunar House one last time and Evie trails after him like his shadow, following him into the study. He inhales its smoky, bookish scent and leans against the mantelpiece.

"I love this room and the people who dwell within," says George looking at Evie, his eyes beginning to fill with tears. There's a fishy tang in the air, and George gives a sad laugh, pointing to limpets Evie has left on the hearth.

George runs his hands along the bookshelves. Evie knows he's savouring the coolness of their leather spines. He tickles Claudette and Florette under their furry chins, and he kneels down to pat Albine, who is sitting on her velvet cushion. He strokes her plump speckled chest. She *burk burks* and the sight of it tugs at Evie's heart.

"I can't remember a happier time in my life, Evie, than the time I've spent here. I pray what I've put into motion will play out the way it should."

Evie stares at George wide-eyed with worry.

"It's all right, Evie. I'm putting things right," whispers George, and Evie notices his chin trembling. She nods, speechless, wanting to ask more, but not having the right words to do so.

George takes one last lingering look at the study and Evie follows him, biting her lip, and doing her best to be brave.

Grandpa and Evie stand arm in arm at the portico of Lunar House, waiting to say goodbye to George. Grandpa's keeping an eye on the front gate, waiting for the bullock dray to arrive from Breamlea. Evie leans into his side and he reaches down for her hand without looking at her. Grandpa has dark shadows under his eyes and Evie's are red and puffy.

The clouds break apart and the sun comes out, making the wet trees and grass glisten.

The coach arrives first, easing to a stop beside them. The driver jumps down, nods at Grandpa and begins to load George's luggage.

Then they hear it. The wheels grinding on gravel, the stomping and snorting of bullocks, the creaking of the dray, the cracking of a whip and loud voices yelling, carrying to them through the bush.

A moment later, the zoo handlers and the bullock dray roll through the gates of Lunar House, pulling up at the stables.

George has heard the bullock dray too and he rushes through the front door, straight past Grandpa and Evie, hurrying to meet the bullock driver and the zoo handlers.

Evie and Grandpa observe the meeting unfolding. The men have their heads bent close together as they talk. The bullock driver starts waving his arms, he shouts and his face turns the colour of a ripe plum. Three of the zoo handlers jump down from the dray and they surround George with hands on their hips, and their faces stony.

"What's going on, Grandpa? Is George in trouble?"

"He's fine, Evie. He's doing fine," says Grandpa, watching the situation through narrowed eyes.

George stands tall and continues to talk. He puts his hand inside his jacket pocket, pulling out a wad of notes, which he passes to the bullock driver and the handlers. The driver gives George a toothless grin and the handlers clap each other on the shoulder before they climb back up onto the dray.

George goes into the stables and closes the door behind him.

Oh, Rhino.

Evie refuses to look, pressing her face into Grandpa's coat. Minutes pass. A high-pitched piping comes from the trees and Evie recognises it as a spinebill – a bird of luck. She remembers Grandpa said "anything is possible when a hummingbird is around", but Evie can't believe in magic today. She snuggles further into Grandpa's side.

Cook and Mr Duffer appear in the doorway behind them. Cook's cheeks are tear-streaked and smudged and Mr Duffer puts his arm around her shoulders.

As the coachman nods to Grandpa to let him know he's done, George returns from the stables.

Evie swallows a lump in her throat.

George moves from foot to foot, as if he's nervous. He trips as he comes forward to kiss Cook goodbye. Composing himself, he shakes hands with Mr Duffer and then he's left standing face-to-face with Grandpa. Evie's heart gives a little lurch. *How close Grandpa and George have become.* George hangs off his every word and Grandpa thrives in George's company.

"Thank you, Charlie. Thank you for everything." George's voice is soft and his face looks much younger. He reaches out and shakes Grandpa's hand, clasping him on the shoulder. Grandpa pulls him in for a hug.

"You're always welcome back here, dear boy."

George nods, his chin beginning to wobble.

Evie's eyes are brimming with tears as George places his hand on the top of her head and ruffles her hair. She catches her breath. She can't say anything; she can't trust herself not to scream.

George bows to them as his coachman opens the door for him.

Evie feels a welling up inside of her, she can't let it go. "Rhino?" she calls to George.

George smiles at Evie and kneels down before her. "Farewell, Evie." He pushes the hair back from her face, kissing her forehead and giving her a reassuring smile.

"Rhino?"

George swings himself up onto the step of the coach and misses, stumbling back to the ground. Cook gasps. He puts his hand up to stop them coming forward to help him and he tries again, this time making it inside the coach. He sits down, removes his hat and pokes his head out of the window.

"*Rhino,*" Evie wails for a third and final time.

Grandpa places his hands on her shoulders.

Evie can feel his hands shaking. She has never known Grandpa to tremble and she starts to cry.

"Rhino?" says George, hanging out of the coach window as it's moving off. "What rhino? I believe an old farmer with poor eyesight mistook a bull seal for a rhinoceros! Have you ever heard of such a thing? I haven't seen *any* rhinoceros."

POST OFFICE TELEGRAPHS, VICTORIA

NO PECUNIARY LIABILITY IS INCURRED BY THE CROWN, BY REASON OF ANY DELAY, DEFAULT, OR OMISSION, IN RELATION TO ANY TELEGRAPHIC MESSAGE SENT OR RECEIVED, OR OMITTED TO BE SENT OR RECEIVED, IN VICTORIA

TO: Royal Melbourne Zoological Society   29th September 1891

Address: Melbourne Post Office

1 Returning	2 to	3 Melbourne	4 forthwith.	5 Stop
6 No	7 rhinoceros	8 found.	9 Stop	10 Believed
11 elderly	12 farmer	13 poor	14 eyesight	15 mistook
16 bull	17 seal	18 for	19 rhinoceros.	20 Stop

from   Master George Henley, C/o Lunar House, Breamlea

CHAPTER 41

As the coach rolls along the driveway, towards the gates of Lunar House, clouds drift and the wind drops to a hush. Evie clings to Grandpa's tweed coat, which smells of all the things she loves, bran and molasses, and smoke and ink.

"What does this mean, Grandpa?" whispers Evie.

"Rhino is staying, Evie," says Grandpa. His face is glowing and his eyes are twinkling and crinkling at the corners.

Grandpa laughs and picks Evie up, swinging her around. "He's staying, Evie. He's staying!" Grandpa is laughing and crying.

Cook and Mr Duffer embrace and they too are laughing and crying at the same time.

"The daft thing is staying, Mr Duffer!"

"We're blessed, Cook. We truly are."

"Can this be true, Grandpa?"

"It is. The unthinkable has happened."

Albine *burk burks* in the portico.

"But why, Grandpa? Why did George leave without Rhino?"

"Because he's our friend, Evie. George has put Rhino's happiness first, our happiness first, ahead of his father, and ahead of the zoo."

Evie is unable to contain herself any longer. She scoops up Albine and dances and twirls. Now she comprehends. Now she understands George. That's why he's been such a mess these last few days. Evie can't imagine what he must have been through to come to this decision, but she is so happy he has. She remembers Gerta, and Grandpa's stolen work and all the pieces of the puzzle. George has set past wrongs to right.

Evie watches the coach pass through the gates. George gives a last wave of his hat out the window and as the coach veers left onto the track, she freezes on the spot. Her mouth drops wide open as there, swinging off the back of the coach, are two cheeky little monkeys.

"Oh, no!" cries Evie.

"How did they git out?" wails Cook.

Evie gapes at Grandpa and Grandpa shoots her a surprised, wide-eyed look. Cook twists a knot in her apron and Mr Duffer's tartan cap falls off.

"Go on, child. Go an' get the bleedin' little devils," says Cook.

Out of the blue, Rhino appears, bellowing. He's somehow got himself out of the stables.

"How did *he* git out?" says Cook, scratching her head.

Grandpa rushes forward and gives Evie a leg-up onto Rhino's back. He takes off like a train, kicking and spraying gravel into the air as he accelerates.

Evie leans forward for balance and she can feel the power in Rhino's hindquarters and he goes faster and faster. They catch up to the coach within a kilometre and gallop alongside until the coach driver sees them.

"Bloomin' heck?!" cries the driver in shock.

"Please, stop!" waves Evie, and he eases the horses to a halt. George pops his head out of the window in alarm.

"What's the matter, Evie? Are you all right?"

"Everything's fine," puffs Evie. Just as she's saying this, Simon somersaults from the roof of the coach. He swings in through the window, landing next to George. Mini leaps from the coach onto Rhino's back, landing behind Evie.

George sits up in surprise, but then he begins to laugh. He holds his hand out to the little monkey and Simon takes it, giving George one of his best gummy grins.

Evie gives George a sheepish grin. She wags her finger at Simon and he hangs his head, knowing he's done the wrong thing.

"What on earth? Evie? They're *rhesus monkeys*?" George doubles over with laughter again.

Evie doesn't know what to say. She's aware she's kept the monkeys a secret and they belong to the zoo, as well as Rhino. She holds her arms out to Simon and he clambers out of the window of the coach, leaping onto Rhino's neck. He moves in to Evie's side, wrapping his arms around her waist.

"I found them hiding in the stables not long before you arrived," says Evie.

George wipes tears from his eyes, but he can't seem to stop himself from laughing. It bubbles up from somewhere deep inside of him. Something catches his eye in the bush and a look of recognition flickers across his face. George bursts out laughing again, quite out of control, thinks Evie.

"There's nothing for me to see here," George says to Evie, smiling at her. He knocks on the roof of the coach. "Drive on, driver. Farewell, dear Evie."

With both little monkeys sitting behind her, Evie breathes a sigh of relief. She watches as George's coach trundles off into the distance.

"Thank you, George," Evie whispers. "Thank you for everything." She stares into the bush where George was gazing and gasps in surprise at some unusual-looking rare white cranes. She's never seen a species such as these before and thinks back to the cargo list from the shipwreck.

It couldn't be?

It couldn't be? Evie shakes her head. But she knows it could be. That dark and light exist in this world. That anything can happen, that things can change and magic is everywhere.

Evie's not sure what this fluttery feeling inside of her is. Hope? Joy? Gratitude? Could it be all three? She laughs. The trees appear greener, the sky is bluer, and the sun feels different upon her face, warming her inside like a generous serve of Cook's apple pie.

"Let's go home, Rhino," says Evie, patting his neck. Rhino flicks his ears and saunters down the track.

✦

Evie and Rhino and the little monkeys ride through the gates of Lunar House, and Grandpa, Cook and Mr Duffer whoop and dance in a circle.

"Three cheers for George!" cries Grandpa.

The celebration soon brings a bounding Francie and Freddie and two sleepy-eyed cats from the study. The ladies appear, running with their wings held high, Albine squawking the loudest. It also brings into the garden a curious old coach horse and a devoted milking cow.

Rhino's ears are swivelling and flicking and his tail twirls in the air. Evie dismounts, wrapping her arms around Rhino's head and he licks her face and snuffles her hair, bellowing. Evie feels the vibrations ripple through her.

"You're staying, Rhino," she whispers into his hairy ears. "You're staying here. For ever."

Grandpa and Cook and Mr Duffer gather around Rhino. Everybody is talking at once, including Simon and Mini, who are chittering and chattering. They admire Rhino's magnificence, his enormous massiveness, his impressively huge horn, his lovely long eyelashes, and his hairy ears. They praise his kindness and gentleness and stroke his neck and scratch his ears.

Rhino bellows loudly. He can't help himself, and he bellows and moos and bellows. It's a contagious feeling. He can feel the energy of the humans around him. It vibrates through the air, vibrates through him. The golden-haired child laughs as she hangs off him. She's glowing with joy, as pure as sunshine after a storm. And he feels they've just come through one. Something significant has happened. And the air is alive. The rippling happiness of the human child ripples through him and he curls his lip, nibbling and snuffling her hair, inhaling her milk and honey sweetness. He can feel the adoration of the adult humans, touching him, patting him and praising him. He knows he's admired, and he stands very still so they can all rub and scratch him at their leisure.

CHAPTER 42

It's spring now and the sun is shining at Lunar House. The roads are dry, the grasses are high and Bream Creek flows sweetly. The bullrushes have multiplied in clumps and dragonflies dart and weave through cat-tail stems.

Birds fill the waterways, which are teeming with swamp hens and ducks and egrets and herons.

On the banks of the creek, golden wattle trees are exploding with fluffy yellow pom pom flowers, and a red flowering gum tree is twittering with budgerigars.

In a dense eucalyptus grove, a pair of orange-bellied parrots squawk and screech as they jostle in taking turns to sit on their clutch of three eggs.

Evie inhales. For the first time in a long time, she feels at peace. She thinks of her mama and papa, but is only remembering the happy things, like how quick Mama was to smile and how often Papa laughed.

Evie can't stop talking and asking Grandpa a million questions. She shouts without meaning to, as if she can't contain herself and Cook scolds, then quickly hugs her.

The aching black grief that filled her has lifted and she feels hungry, her appetite filling out her hollow cheeks and bird-like limbs. Evie feels full of conversation and life. Life at Lunar House. Life with dear Rhino.

"Grandpa, when can I go back to school?"

"Evie, my dear girl, I've been hoping you'd wish to return. That's wonderful news. I'll make the necessary arrangements and Mr Duffer can drive you in on Monday."

Rhino spends his days grazing in the company of Dominique and Bernard. He hangs out with the ladies, and sniffle snuffles Claudette and Florette. He plays chase with Francie and Freddie and lets Simon and Mini ride around on his back.

He continues to be helpful around the farm, assisting Cook with hanging out the washing and Mr Duffer with any heavy lifting duties.

Evie and Rhino enjoy their daily walks exploring the beach and the paddocks, spending hours down at the creek. Evie sketches birds and watches Rhino swim and roll around his wallow.

She often talks to Rhino about George Henley and she's sure Rhino understands her every word. Evie knows George would have returned to Melbourne to have it out with his father. But George was ready, he now knows how strong he is.

Without a doubt, Grandpa and George's regular letter correspondence indicates that George is weathering the storm.

Grandpa and Mr Duffer make plans to repair the roof of Lunar House and to tidy up the garden, starting with pruning the rose arbour. Evie thinks Grandma Amelie would be proud to see her garden returning to its former glory.

Grandpa has finished his scientific research paper about the near-extinct orange-bellied parrot and it has been accepted for publication by the newly formed Ornithological Society of Victoria.

✦

A day before Christmas, Paddy Tait arrives with an impressive-looking delivery for Mr Charles Strahan. Evie can see it's a heavy parcel, bearing the gold crest of the Royal Melbourne Zoological Society.

"It looks important," says Paddy, who hardly needs an excuse to lock up early to visit Lunar House.

They crowd around the kitchen table as Grandpa unwraps the package. Evie and Cook gasp, clasping their hands together as Grandpa promptly sits down.

There, before them in all its magnificence, is a brand-new copy of a beautiful, green leather-bound book. It's the latest edition of *The Birds of Australia* by C.H. Strahan and D.L. Henley.

"What is the bleedin' thing?" says Paddy.

"Oh, Paddy. Didn't yer know our Mr Strahan 'ere is a famous orni ... orno logical ... birdman? He's famous, I'm telling yer now," says Cook.

"An orni what?" says Paddy.

"Ornithologist, Paddy," says Evie. "It means Grandpa is an expert in the scientific study of birds."

Paddy's eyes widen and he nods as Grandpa strokes the green leather cover.

"Thank goodness our George called his father out for what he is," says Cook.

Grandpa gives Cook a stern look.

"Well ... he's nothin' but a bully and a thief, he is."

"All right now, Cook, that will do," says Grandpa, laughing.

Grandpa smiles at Evie and she beams back at him, with a grin from ear to ear.

"I have no doubt you've had a hand in this, Evie. My dearest Evie."

Evie gazes out the window at Rhino, her heart

full at the turn of events in their lives – all because of a rhinoceros, a very special rhinoceros.

"Oh, no, quick. Something's burnin'!" says Cook, rushing to the oven.

Cook's been busy cooking and preparing for Christmas lunch, as this year everyone is invited, including Cook and Mr Duffer, and George, who is due to arrive shortly. He's just signing off on a lease for his new restaurant, Henley's Fine Dining, in Geelong.

CHAPTER 43

Rhino awakens to the crisp freshness of a new day. He tilts his head and inhales many delectable smells. The fuggy cowness of Dominique and the feathery pungency of the ladies, both of which make him immensely happy.

Then there's the aroma and the delightful rankness of the warm straw upon which they lay. The richness of bran and molasses, the mustiness of the stables, the smell of dubbin on leather and the sweet tang of fresh horse manure.

He takes his time to rise, farting with the effort. Upon standing, he sways and arches his back, stretching out one leg at a time. He swirls his tail and saunters to the door of the stables. Yawning loudly, with a great huff of grassy morning breath, he nudges the door open with his horn.

On the breeze he can smell the loamy richness of dirt and the divine stink of the wallow. He can smell worms, swamp hens and yams. And dogs, silly dogs. He can smell the sharp urine of cats, the reek of monkeys and the sweetness of new shoots of growth. Then he smells her, the familiar milk and honey sweetness of the golden-haired child. The small human called Evie. His Evie.

His heart lifts. He knows today will be another day of wonder, full of walking and exploring and staring at clouds drifting across the sky. It will be a day of licking rain from clover leaves and nuzzling and huffling with Dominique. It will be a day of birdwatching and wallowing in cool silky black mud and of ear scratches and of all things Evie.

Rhino hasn't thought of his old home for a while now; and if he does, it doesn't hurt as much as it used to. This place, this special place – like the place he has in his heart for Evie – is his home. Evie is home.

He can hear her footfalls as she comes to him now, as quiet as the night. Sleepy-eyed and tussle-haired, she leans into him. With desperation she clasps his head as only she does, staring at him with a deep intensity. Her little hands scratch behind his ears. She whispers things he doesn't understand, but he knows in his heart their meaning by the rise and fall of her voice. She's like a little bird. His little bird. His tummy rumbles with contentment as he lowers his nose to snuffle her hair to wish her, too, a good morning.

29th September 1891

Dear Sir,

I apologise for the delay in my correspondence.

Unfortunately, I have bad news for the Royal Zoological Society.

There is no rhinoceros at Breamlea. There never was. I believe an elderly farmer saw a bull seal in the shallows and imagined it to be a rhinoceros.

I would like to take this opportunity to inform you I will not be returning to work for you, nor for the Royal Zoological Society.

I am not certain about what the future holds for me, but, for once in my life, I will determine it for myself and I am excited at the prospect.

There is one other delicate matter I must raise. It is in regards to the next edition of your self-proclaimed book *The Birds of Australia*. Let me make this clear, Father – the next reprint will in no uncertain terms acknowledge the joint authorship of you and C.H. Strahan. If you refuse these terms, I shall be forced to expose your dishonesty, which I can assure you will result in your public humiliation and disgrace.

I bid you farewell.
Your son,
George Henley

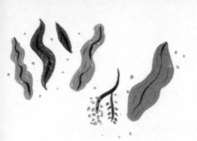

AUTHOR'S NOTE

The steamship *SS Bancoora* was driven ashore at Breamlea in the south-west of Victoria by heavy seas on 14 July 1891. It left Calcutta on 9 June with a full load of tea, rice, tapioca, sugar and jute. There was also an unusual cargo load of exotic animals bound for the Royal Melbourne Zoo: a young elephant, a rhinoceros, six rhesus monkeys, two white cranes and six green parrots.

As they rounded Cape Otway at 2 a.m., a south-easterly gale-force wind hit the *SS Bancoora* and it was run aground on a reef eight hundred metres from shore.

Unbeknown to the crew, a local farmer, a Mr Milne, heard the calls of distress but was unable to cross a flooded creek to reach the beach, so he rode his horse to Geelong to raise the alarm.

WRECK OF THE STEAMSHIP BANCOORA. Drawn from a Photograph by J. R. Mann, C.E.—(see page 22.)

IMAGE: STATE LIBRARY OF VICTORIA

The *SS Bancoora* remained stranded on the reef until 28 August when salvagers were able to get access and set up a pontoon and winching system to bring the animals ashore. The animals were then taken on to the Melbourne Zoo. Sadly, the rhinoceros only lived for a short time before dying of a back injury sustained during the shipwreck.

ENTELLUS MONKEYS

WHITE IBIS

RHINOCEROS

SECRATARY BIRDS

WHITE CRANE

YOUNG ALBATROSS

BABY LION and TIGER

THE ADDITIONS TO THE ZOO.—[SEE PAGE 22].

IMAGE: STATE LIBRARY OF VICTORIA

Upon reading a true account in TROVE at the National Library of Australia, I wasn't sure what upset me the most – the preposterous idea of exotic animal acquisition by zoos, or the thought of animals suffering, who survive the shipwreck only to go into a life in captivity. This story would not let me go.

I have stood on these same windswept beaches. I have combed its shores. It's rugged and bleak and isolated, and I could see the ship being smashed upon the reef and I could hear the wailing of the animals.

I mourned for the loss of the rhinoceros, a truly misunderstood creature, and it was my admiration for them that inspired me to write this story and ask the "what if" questions.

What if the rhinoceros washed ashore? What if a girl, who walked the beach every day, found the exhausted rhinoceros asleep in the shallows and led it home by the horn? What if this girl, named Evie, formed an immediate bond with the rhinoceros? A connection so strong it had the power to heal?

This story became very real to me, and it's most certainly me walking in Evie's shoes. I grew up on a farm doing chores every day and we were flooded in every winter when the creek burst her banks. I've tramped every inch of the beach and our farm.

Rhino is a three-year-old Indian rhinoceros from northern India, also known as the greater one-horned rhinoceros. So, yes, they only have one horn, differing from their African cousins, who have two.

Over the centuries, the rhinoceros has built a reputation for being aggressive. This is because they have poor eyesight and may charge upon an unfamiliar smell. They have even been known to attack rocks and trees, but left unprovoked they are peaceful, placid animals.

But it is no wonder they're angry at times! Poachers are hunting rhinos to near extinction for their horns, which are made of keratin, like

1ère série. QUADRUPÈDES aux os marsupiaux (L. G. série)

6ème Ordre
PACHYDERMES.   Rhinocéros des Indes. (Rhinoceros indicus, Cuv.) De la grande mod.

fingernails and hair. They are prized as weapons, and coveted as an ingredient in traditional Asian medicine.

Hand-raised as an orphan, my Rhino is gentle and docile. He loves chin scratches and ear tickles and munching on green grass, preferably after a light drizzling of rain. He's quick to smile and bestow kisses on any unsuspecting human he deems worthy. He's passionate about cows, adores the company of chickens and loves to wallow in mud.

Rhino is most definitely the hero of this story.

This story questions and addresses the importance and beauty in the connection between humans and animals and the profound healing love animals inspire and give to us. I hope this love shines through in *Evie and Rhino*.

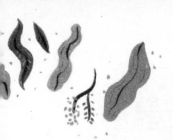

SHIPWRECK COAST

The coastline from Cape Otway to Portland in south-west Victoria is known as the Shipwreck Coast. There are 638 known shipwrecks along this stretch of rugged coast, although only around 240 of them have been discovered. This treacherous coastline is marred by hidden reefs, shifting sand bars, strong currents and rips and wildly unpredictable gale-force storms.

COOK'S DELICIOUS APPLE PIE RECIPE

YOU WILL NEED

For the pastry
255 grams plain flour
pinch of salt
140 grams butter
6 teaspoons cold water

For the filling
3 large Bramley cooking apples, sliced
sugar, to taste
Pie dish 20 cm diameter

METHOD

1. Preheat the oven to 180 °C.
2. Sieve the flour and salt into a bowl.
3. Rub in the butter until the mixture resembles breadcrumbs.
4. Add water to the flour and mix with your hands. The pastry should be of an even colour and consistency for rolling.
5. Divide the pastry into two halves. Take one half and roll it out so that it is big enough to cover a 20-cm pie dish. Trim the edges with a knife using the edge of the pie dish as your guide.
6. Cover the pastry with the sliced apples and sprinkle with sugar.
7. Roll out the other half of the pastry. Moisten the edge of the bottom layer of pastry and place the second piece on top.
8. Trim off any excess pastry with a knife in a downward motion, again using the edge of the pie dish as your guide.
9. Flute the edges with a pinching action using your fingers and thumb.
10. Prick the surface of the pastry lightly before placing the pie in the oven. Cook for 20 to 30 minutes at 180 °C.
11. Serve, dusted with caster sugar and a dollop of cream.

ABOUT THE AUTHOR

Neridah McMullin grew up on a farm surrounded by a menagerie of animals. When she wasn't on the farm, she was at their holiday home on the south-west coast of Victoria, beachcombing, exploring and swimming. Neridah is the author of eight books for children and she loves animals, Australian history and true stories. Her latest picture book, *Drover*, released in 2021, celebrates legendary drover, Edna Jessop. Neridah loves reading and writing and footy and cricket. She also loves rhinoceroses, monkeys and birdwatching.

ACKNOWLEDGEMENTS

My heartfelt thanks to the wonderful team at Walker Books Australia. A big thank you to Linsay Knight, for her belief and encouragement, and to my editor, Christina Pagliaro, for making this book the best it could be.

Thank you to Astred Hicks, for her beautiful illustrations and design.

Thank you to Sue Whiting, for her exceptional editorial guidance, and to Alison Arnold, who has helped me enormously over the years. Thank you to all my "Bernie" friends from the Lake House Writers Retreat.

To my wonderful family, who hold me up. To my parents, John and Lynette Bade, who've always told me I can do anything. To my grandparents, long gone, but never forgotten, all of whom dearly loved all animals.

To my husband, Ian, who makes all things possible, and still tears up when he proofreads my work.

Thank you to my beautiful children and their chosen ones: Lach and Jas, Josh and Mimi, and to Toby, my ray of sunshine and the king of interruption. But he did say he'd love to read a story about a rhinoceros in a shipwreck.

To my brother, Roger, with whom I shared the perfect childhood. To my sister-in-law, Angela, and my nephews, Connor and Angus, for their constant love.

Thank you to the entire McMullin family – they're a big family!

Thank you to my children's writing community: SCBWI, the Duck Pond and to CBCA. You're the best, keeping me sane, centred and inspired.

And lastly, to all the little children who save lost creatures, keep doing it. And to all animals out there, ugly or otherwise, you are loved.

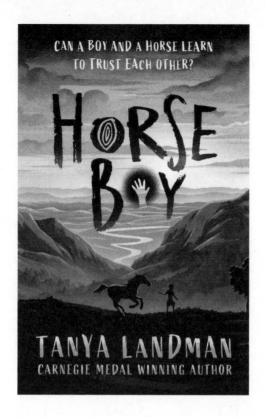

A boy without a clan. A hunted animal.
Can they survive together?

Oak is finally old enough to join the hunt, but nothing is as it should be – the rains have failed, a strange mood has overtaken his father, and now he must face these mysterious new creatures called horses.

Then Oak becomes separated from his clan with only a distressed young horse for company, and it seems that things could get no worse. But perhaps not all animals are prey.
Perhaps Horse can be clan, too?

"A happy addition to the shelf of child-animal friendship stories."
The Times